Dear Reader,

In 2009, I attended my first ever RWA National Conference in beautiful Washington, D.C. It was so amazing to meet other authors in person who I'd only previously known online, to soak up workshops and attend parties. I reconnected with my good friend Fiona Harper, and on a gorgeous summer evening we met up with Shirley Jump and sat on an outdoor patio at a Thai restaurant, noshing on summer rolls and soup, talking a mile a minute.

Over dinner, the idea of this trilogy was born. It took a while for us to sort out our schedules, but we were delighted to get the green light. I can't tell you how wonderful it is to work on a project with two women who are not only great writers but great friends. We're all from different countries, we all have our own writing style, but there's something that unites us all as well as the three McKinnon sisters in our stories—love and forgiveness and healing. All wrapped up in a Christmas bow.

There's something special about writing a holiday story—maybe because Christmas is one of my favorite times of year. Hope McKinnon is definitely in need of some Christmas magic. Fortunately, Blake Nelson has an abundant supply that he's more than willing to share. And maybe, just maybe, there'll be a little holiday miracle for both of them.

Wishing you the very best this holiday season,

Donna

DONNA ALWARD

Sleigh Ride with the Rancher

HARLEQUIN®

entertain, enrich, inspire™

Recycling programs
for this product may
not exist in your area.

ISBN-13: 978-0-373-17843-8

SLEIGH RIDE WITH THE RANCHER

First North American Publication 2012

Copyright © 2012 by Donna Alward

busy wife and mother of three (two daughters and the family dog), **Donna Alward** believes hers is the best job in the world: a combination of stay-at-home mom and romance novelist. An avid reader since childhood, Donna always made up her own stories. She completed her arts degree in English literature in 1994, but it wasn't until 2001 that she penned her first full-length novel and found herself hooked on writing romance. In 2006 she sold her first manuscript, and now writes warm, emotional stories for Harlequin® Romance.

In her new home office in Nova Scotia, Donna loves being back on the east coast of Canada after nearly twelve years in Alberta, where her career began, writing about cowboys and the West. Donna's debut romance, *Hired by the Cowboy,* was awarded the Bookseller's Best Award in 2008 for Best Traditional Romance.

With the Atlantic Ocean only minutes from her doorstep, Donna has found a fresh take on life and promises even more great romances in the near future!

Donna loves to hear from readers. You can contact her through her website, www.donnaalward.com, her page at www.myspace.com/dalward, or through her publisher.

Books by Donna Alward

THE REBEL RANCHER
THE LAST REAL COWBOY
HOW A COWBOY STOLE HER HEART
A FAMILY FOR THE RUGGED RANCHER
HONEYMOON WITH THE RANCHER

Other titles by this author available in ebook format.

CHAPTER ONE

THE cold air penetrated clear through Hope McKinnon's jacket as she stepped out of the rented car and looked up at the home base of the Bighorn Therapeutic Riding Facility. It was December in Alberta yet it felt like the arctic! It was a shock to her system after she'd reluctantly left the hot brilliance of the Sydney sun only hours before.

She huddled into her woolen coat and popped the trunk for her bag. The wheels of her suitcase squeaked and dragged on the snow covering the path to the wrap-around porch of the big log home. Coming up the long lane, she'd thought it had a fairy-tale quality, like a romantic ski chalet nestled in the mountains. Twinkling fairy lights were intertwined through evergreen boughs on the railing, glowing softly in the waning light of late afternoon.

But that had been in the warm car, with the heater going full blast. Now she shivered. The house was rapidly losing its winter magic as she gave the case a tug over a ridge of packed-down snow. She heaved it up the stairs one at a time, growing more and more irritated until she plunked it down beside her leg and rang the doorbell.

Three times.

She huddled into her jacket as she waited.

By this time her legs were cold and her feet were beginning to go numb in the soft leather boots she wore. She looked around and saw a truck parked next to the barn. She was supposed to meet a man named Blake Nelson, the guy who ran the ranch. She'd been guilt-tripped by her grandmother into coming and taking pictures of his operation, and she wasn't all that pleased about it. She could think of a million other places she'd rather be in December than in the icy cold of Alberta.

But she was here, and she was freezing, so she left her suitcase by the door and made her way across the yard toward the barn. A light glowed from a window within, a warm beacon against the grayness of the afternoon shadows. It would be warm inside, wouldn't it? She quickened her step as she neared the door.

The next thing she knew she was slightly airborne as her boot hit a piece of ice camouflaged by a skiff of snow. The weightless sensation lasted only a second and was immediately followed by a bone-jarring, breath-stealing thump as she landed squarely on her rump.

"Ow!" she cried out as her tailbone struck frozen ground. She fought for a few moments as her emptied lungs struggled for air, and then gasped it in painfully, closing her eyes.

When she opened them she was looking at a pair of worn leather cowboy boots that disappeared into two very long, denim-clad legs. Humiliation burned up her neck and into her cheeks as she forgot the pain in her bottom. What a way to make a first impression!

"You must be Hope," said a warm, deep voice with just the barest hint of a drawl. "Let me give you a hand up."

The rich voice sent shivers down her spine and she struggled to keep her breath even. She looked up then, and couldn't help the gasp that escaped her lips. This Blake guy—assuming it was him—was stunning. Incredibly tall, and the form he cut was that of the quintessential cowboy, complete with sheepskin jacket and a dark brown cowboy hat to match. His breath made white puffs in the wintry air.

Her photographer's eye was already framing him as if she were behind the lens, capturing him like a great Western icon.

"Did you hit your head or something?" He still held out his hand and she realized she'd been staring at him like he was the eighth wonder of the world.

"Sorry," she said, holding up her hand and grasping his wrist. He gave a quick tug and she was on her feet again. She hid her flaming face by twisting and brushing the snow off her pants and the tails of her jacket. She didn't stand much hope of dignity now. She might as well make the best of it.

"You have to watch out for the odd bit of ice in the yard," he cautioned. "Those boots don't look like they have much tread. I hope you brought something heavier."

She tried to ignore the humiliation that seemed to burn her cheeks at his chastising tone, making her feel foolish and about five years old. She lifted her eyes and tilted her head to look up, studying his profile as he turned to inspect her heeled boots.

The looking up was a rarity. At five-foot-ten, and with a modest two-inch heel, she stood an even six feet. And she still had to look up at Blake Nelson. He had to be at least six-four, six-five. Most of the time she felt like an ungainly giant, but next to his strong build she felt positively feminine. Or she would, except she could still feel the bump on her butt, reminding her of her grand entrance. Perfect.

He turned his head slightly so he faced her squarely, and the part of his face which had been shadowed by his hat was now clearly visible. Her heart seemed to drop to her toes, and a small cry escaped her lips before she could stop it.

For the space of several heartbeats she was back in the hospital again, trying terribly hard to look at her best friend Julie in the face as the bandages came off. To smile when she felt like weeping; to tell Julie it wasn't that bad when in truth the raw shock and ugliness of her friend's injuries had made her sick to her stomach. The same queasiness threatened now and she gulped in air, needing to steady herself. This cowboy wasn't so perfect, after all. A long scar ran from his right temple clear to his jaw—pink, ugly, and puckered.

"Are you sure you're okay? You've gone quite pale."

The words were polite but Hope was aware enough to realize how very cold they were. He knew exactly what had happened. She'd taken one look at the mess that was his right cheek and she'd been repulsed. What he didn't understand was why and she was too fragile right now to explain it. The last thing she wanted to do was break down in front of a stranger.

There wasn't a day went by that Hope didn't see Julie's smiling face in her mind and feel the hole that her death had left behind. Julie had been the most beautiful girl Hope had ever known—beautiful inside and out. It had been six months since her funeral, but Hope couldn't get the image of Julie's ravaged body out of her head. It had all been so unfair, especially since Julie had been the one person Hope had let herself get close to in all these years. Julie had understood about Hope's family, about her dysfunction and frustration and the futility of hoping that someday it would all work out.

And then Julie, like everyone else in Hope's life, had abandoned her. Not by choice. Hope knew that. But when she was alone in the apartment they'd shared, when there was no one to text during a slow workday, or catch a drink with on an outdoor patio, it felt like the same thing.

Hope fought for control and shut the feelings down before they overwhelmed her completely. She had to keep focus.

"I'm Hope," she announced, trying desperately to sound normal. It shouldn't matter that he'd been injured and left disfigured. Except that it really did. It smashed into the concrete wall she'd put around her feelings with all the subtlety of a wrecking ball, reminding her of everything she'd rather forget.

"Blake," he replied, but the coolness remained in his tone. "And I'm guessing you're pretty cold right about now. Let's get you up to the house."

As they walked back to the house she was constantly aware of his hand by her elbow, waiting to catch her if she slipped again. It was courteous, considering their shaky start, but unsettling, too. He opened the door—unlocked, making her feel foolish once again—and held it for her to enter before grabbing her suitcase as if it weighed nothing at all and bringing it inside.

She almost wept in relief at the blast of heat that greeted her, and forgot about all her reservations at staying in a private home. She could think about that later. Right now she would focus on warming up and that was all that mattered.

He started up the stairs with her case. "I've got your room ready. I put you on the west side of the house. I thought you'd like that. It's got a view of the mountains, and the early-morning sun won't bother you. Not that it rises that early this time of year."

He was being terribly polite, and Hope was beginning to feel doubly guilty about her obvious reaction to his face, half wanting to explain and half wanting just to forget all about it and start over.

"Thanks," she said, injecting as much warmth as she could into the word. "I'm pretty jet-lagged. I'm lucky I know which end is up."

He stopped in front of a door and opened it, but his closed expression told her he hadn't exactly thawed toward her yet. "You can always nap for a while if you want," he offered. "I've got chores to finish up in the barn."

He was getting away from her as fast as he could, she realized, her heart sinking. So much for starting over.

She considered taking a nap, but she knew it would probably be better if she stayed up awhile longer and tried to go to bed later, so she didn't end up being as nocturnal as a koala.

"I think I'll wait a while, try to adjust."

She stepped into the bedroom and momentarily reconsidered. The rustic cabin-style decor in what she'd seen of the house was repeated in this room, with knotty pine paneling climbing the steeply pitched walls. Along the center of the outside wall, lined up with the peak of the pitch, was a heavy wooden bed that looked like it had been hewn from logs. It was covered in a gorgeous raspberry-and-cream quilt with several fluffy pillows on the top.

While definitely not her personal decorating taste, Hope found the room surprisingly cozy and welcoming. She could hardly wait to sink into the softness of the mattress, snuggle beneath that quilt with her head cushioned on the pillows. A stone gas fireplace was tucked in one corner. Hope almost swooned with pleasure. All it would take was a flick of a switch and she'd have toasty flames to heat up the room.

Blake put down her suitcase as she went to the window and looked out. For miles the white foothills rolled, leading to the gray hulking shapes of the Rockies—so large that they appeared closer than she suspected they actually were. In all her travels around the world as a photographer she'd never been here, and she suspected that on a clear, crisp day the white-capped peaks were stunning.

She turned and chafed her hands together. "Thanks. Mr. Nelson..."

"Just Blake," he corrected, straightening. "I'm not so much into formality around here."

"Blake," she continued, unsure how she felt about him calling her Hope instead of Ms. McKinnon for the duration of her visit. The last thing she needed was anyone getting overly personal. She preferred to keep her distance, after all. "Doesn't this feel weird to you? A stranger in your home?"

He looked taken aback by her question. "You city people," he said. "It's not like that around here. Consider it Western hospitality."

The words should have been friendly, but to Hope they still held the stiff veneer of politeness. Great. So he was as awkward about her being here as she was. She should have stood her ground and told Gram no. But she'd never been able to say no to Gram...

Hope considered telling him she hadn't always been a city girl. She'd spent lots of time climbing trees and swimming and picking wildflowers. Getting grass stains and skinned knees from falling off her bike, and in a town where you could knock on anyone's door for a quick glass of water or a Band-Aid to heal a scrape. The memories caused a pang inside. They hadn't been ideal yesterdays but they weren't all bad, especially all the times spent in Beckett's Run with Gram. That town was about as far from a big city as you could get.

She looked up at him, smiled politely, and kept her mouth shut.

He shrugged. "After what Mary said on the phone, there's no trouble with you staying here. Really."

Hope's brow furrowed. What did Blake mean? The only reason she was here was to take pictures, right? She replayed her conversation with Gram in her head. *Pictures and...*

Something uncomfortable wound its way through Hope's chest. *Pictures and down time,* Gram had said. Time spent not working. In a house with a single man...

Gram wouldn't be matchmaking, would she?

Hope banished the thought. Gram didn't even *know* Blake. The very idea was ridiculous. Boy, Hope really did need some sleep, didn't she?

She looked into Blake's face and thought she saw his eyes soften with what looked like compassion. Compassion for her? Ridiculous. "I don't know what she told you. Why don't you enlighten me?"

At her sharp tone the soft look in his eyes disappeared and she wondered if she'd imagined it. He tilted his head the slightest bit, his keen gaze feeling a bit like an assessment as he paused.

He shook his head. "You look dead on your feet. We can talk about things later, after you've had a chance to rest and have something to eat. I've got to get back out to the barn, but I'll put on some coffee in the kitchen before I go."

He looked down at her legs and back up again, his expression knowing. His examination made her feel about two inches tall.

"If I were you I'd change out of your wet pants. The snow is starting to melt. You're going to be quite uncomfortable in about thirty seconds."

She looked down and saw a puddle by her boots. She

hadn't taken them off when she came inside. Hadn't done anything but march dutifully up the stairs. She looked back up, but her head seemed to lag half a second behind her eyes. Uh-oh. Having the equivalent of an out-of-body experience was no time for a conversation about the whys and wherefores of the next few weeks. It would keep.

"Coffee would be great, thank you."

He went to leave but turned back, his right cheek facing her so she couldn't look at him without seeing the scar in all its angry, beastly detail. The funny tingling sensation she recognized as anxiety crawled down the backs of her legs again but she forced herself to hold his gaze.

"I'll be back inside at dinner. Anna put a roast in the crockpot this morning, so we can eat when I come back."

Anna? Hope felt a rush of relief. Perhaps they weren't going to be alone, then. Maybe Gram had been wrong. Maybe Blake had a wife, or a girlfriend.

That would be very welcome news, because while Hope certainly lived in the twenty-first century, there was a small part of her that felt odd knowing it was just going to be the two of them under the same roof.

Wouldn't her friends have a chuckle about *that?* Who knew she would be so *traditional,* after all? Of course she might just be feeling that way because, despite the scar and the cool attitude, she did find Blake rather attractive in a raw, rugged sort of way...

"Is Anna your wife? Girlfriend?"

He grinned then, and the sight of it changed his face completely, making her catch her breath.

"That'd give her a laugh," he chuckled. "Anna's my part-time housekeeper. You'll meet her tomorrow."

He stepped back and touched the brim of his hat, a gallant gesture that took her by surprise.

"Make yourself at home. I'll be back in a few hours.

And, Hope?" The momentary smile was wiped away as he frowned, and his face was all planes and angles again. "Get some rest before you fall over again."

His boots clomped down the stairs and she heard the front door slam.

She sat to take off her boots and her pants chafed against her legs.

Dammit, he was right. About the pants, the falling over—all of it.

And it was probably a very good thing that she was too tired to care. It was going to be a very long ten days.

CHAPTER TWO

BLAKE opened the gate and brought the horses from the corral. Each one plodded to its own stall, where it was warm and where fresh flakes of hay and water waited. A storm was brewing. Blake could feel it in the air—a blend of moisture and expectation that he recognized after living his whole life in the shadow of the Rockies. The gray cloud cover that had made the day so bleak and the air raw was bringing snow. This close to the mountains it was bound to get ugly.

It was a good thing Hope had arrived when she had.

He closed up the stall doors and frowned. His grandmother had called after it had all been set up, and then Hope's grandmother had followed up, calling him personally. He'd said yes to Hope staying here for one reason only: because Mary had promised that Hope would take pictures for him, providing professional shots to be used on the facility's website and in promo materials for organizations all over western Canada. He appreciated the favor because money was tight and he tried to put every cent he could back into the facility. Bighorn needed a better professional presence, and he wasn't going to get it with a few snapshots and a website he'd put together from a template. He knew where his strengths were. IT support wasn't it.

But then Mary had insinuated that Hope was in desperate need of a holiday, too, that she was really struggling and a place like his was just what she needed.

He'd tried to ignore that last part because he had no desire to get personally involved. It was uncomfortable enough having her stay in the house with him, but what else could he do? Say no and ship her off to a hotel miles away? His mother would have something to say about that and the Western hospitality he'd been sure to point out to Hope just minutes ago. He'd resigned himself to having a house guest, and made sure that Anna had prepared the guestroom for her in welcome.

But he hadn't expected a tall, elegant blonde with sleek hair and the slightest lilt of an acquired Australian accent to show up. She was the kind of girl who, in his high school days, had intimidated the hell out of him. The kind of girl who wore the best clothes and hung with the cool people and looked down her nose at guys like Blake. Guys who were less than perfect. He'd had her pegged the moment he saw the expensive high-heeled boots and the stylish scarf looped around her neck in some crazy, fashionable knot.

She'd hooked her hand into his and he'd felt the contact straight to his belt buckle as he helped her to her feet. Before he'd even been able to put the reaction into perspective she'd looked into his face.

He'd seen that look before. Revulsion. Disgust. Over the years he'd grown more patient with people. He knew the scar was ugly. Shocking, even. And the reactions were just that—reactions. People naturally expected a perfect face, and his was anything but. He never faulted anyone for a moment's reaction. So why did Hope's make him scowl so?

Maybe because she'd been worse than the others. Not surprise or a small wince before glancing away. She'd ac-

tually paled and swayed on her feet. His pride had taken
a hit and he'd heard the echoes of his school nickname in
his head… *Hey, Beast.* The *Beauty and the Beast* movie
had been out a few years earlier than his accident and all
the girls remembered the words from the songs, taunting
him with them through the hallways when the teachers
weren't paying attention.

There was nothing he could do about his disfigurement.
Nor had they understood the fact that the pain of it was
nothing compared to the agony of losing his twin, Brad.

Enough time had passed now that the memories had
become a part of who he was, so intrinsically a part of him
that he usually forgot all about it. But not today. Today
he was off his stride and *she'd* shown up with her supe-
rior airs, making it sound like he wouldn't want her here
when it was clear that *she* was the one who would rather
be somewhere else. It was only his sense of hospitality
and the promise he'd made his grandmother that had kept
him from answering with the words that had hovered on
his tongue.

His mother had raised him to be a gentleman, after all.
And so by the time he'd got Hope's suitcase to her room
he'd calmed his temper and attempted pleasantness.

He shut the last stall door and slid the bolt home with
a loud *thunk.* Before he left he ventured into the storage area of the barn and ran his fingers over the wood
of the sleigh he'd bought from a rancher near Nanton.
It was old, but solid. The green paint had been chipped
when it was delivered. Now it was stripped and sanded,
the runners reinforced, and the whole thing waited to be
repainted. He'd been planning this for a while, keeping
his eye out for a used sleigh he could refinish—one big
enough to seat a driver upfront and a group of kids in the
back. A group of kids who needed help making the kind

of Christmas memories that Blake had known growing up. The kind that came with hot cocoa and cookies and visits from Santa Claus.

It shouldn't bother him that a look of surprise and aversion had touched Hope's face. He had more important things to think about. But it irritated him just the same. His hands moved over the gentle curves of the wood as he considered, picturing her flawless skin, her waterfall of soft hair, her sweetly curved body... She was tall and long-limbed and, despite being jet-lagged, moved with an innate grace he admired.

Maybe he'd been working with physical disabilities too long if he could make that complete an assessment of her based on a five-minute acquaintance.

As usual, working with the animals helped him sort out his thoughts. While the ranch catered for children with visible disabilities, he was well aware that not all problems could be seen by the naked eye. He dedicated his life to helping people look beyond the scars and disabilities of others. Not a day went by that he didn't think of Brad and how they'd planned a life that was no longer a possibility. It was the driving force behind Bighorn Therapeutic Riding, after all.

Maybe, just maybe, he owed that same courtesy to Hope. If he didn't, he'd be as closed-minded as all the people who had turned away from him over the years. So, he mused, as he turned out the barn lights and closed the door, he'd put his first impressions of Hope aside and give her the benefit of the doubt.

It was silent inside the house, and for a minute Blake wondered if Hope had taken a nap. She'd been dead on her feet, her eyes slightly unfocused as she'd stared at him in her room. The scent of roasting meat, garlic and bay leaves permeated the hall from the kitchen and his stomach growled. Should he wake her for dinner or save her a plate?

And then he found Hope sitting at the breakfast counter, laptop open, her delicately arched brows wrinkled in the middle as she focused on something on the screen, prissy little glasses perched on her nose. The stylish kind of spectacles that looked more like an accessory than anything else.

"So, not asleep, after all?"

She started at the sound of his voice. "Oh, goodness!"

"You didn't hear me come in?"

"I tend to block things out when I'm editing," she explained, tucking a silky sheet of her hair behind her ear. "Sorry."

"Editing?"

"Of course. I find the imperfections in the pictures and then work to make them better. Come look," she said, turning the laptop a few degrees so he could see the screen better.

He was off step again, expecting one thing and finding another. He'd been about to apologize for his earlier coolness and here she was looking refreshed and businesslike, as if things hadn't been awkward at all.

He went to the counter and peered over her shoulder.

The picture was of a female model, posed in a white overcoat and stilettos, her hair artfully blowing around her face.

"Looks good," he said. Truthfully, it looked a bit sterile and lifeless. There was too much white and the model looked like she might be blown away with the first stiff breeze to ruffle her umbrella. With her hair blowing like that, and a coat on, he would've expected an outdoor shot rather than…what? It looked like she was standing inside a cube. Why would she need an umbrella in a cube?

"Let me show you the original." She brought up another picture and put them both side by side. "See?"

Her smile was wide and expectant as he looked at the screen again. Honestly, he couldn't see much difference.

"You're clearly a pro," he commented, stepping back.

Her brows knit closer together. "Don't you see? Look right here." She pointed to the model's jaw. "This line is totally different now. And that spot?"

He had to lean right in to see where she indicated.

"It's gone in this one. And I lightened everything just a bit as the exposure wasn't quite right. It's totally different. Now it's nearly perfect."

"And perfection is important?"

She looked at him like he'd suddenly sprouted an extra head. "Of course," she chattered. "I mean, I'm always looking for the perfect shot. That's what I do. I haven't found it yet, but I will someday." Her lips took on a determined set. "Until then I keep trying, and I tweak and fix what I have. It's so different than in the old days, before digital."

Perfection. His mood soured. If she was looking for perfection, boy, was she in the wrong place.

"Yeah, well, I've always been a point-and-shoot kind of guy."

He went to the counter next to the sink and took the cover off the Crock-pot. Steam and scent assaulted him and he breathed deeply. No one did elk roast like Anna.

"Dinner's in ten—I'm going to make some gravy," he said, taking out a large platter.

He put the roast in the center and scooped out potatoes, carrots and golden chunks of turnip, arranging them around the roast. Then he tented them all with foil while he poured the broth into a saucepan and set it to heat, mixing flour and water to thicken it. He marveled at the change in her. Not only had she traded her wet clothes for dry, but the dazed look in her eyes was gone and she seemed full of chatter. Like she was two entirely different people. Which one was the real Hope?

The chatter was annoying on one hand but somehow pleasant on the other. The house often felt too quiet with just him here in the winter months. He supposed that one of these days he should get off his butt and think about having a family of his own.

And yet every time he considered it something held him back. Something he didn't want to examine too closely. Things were better the way they were now.

"Mr. Nelson?"

He paused, his hand on the flour bin. "It's Blake, remember?"

"I just… I want to apologize for earlier. I think we got off on the wrong foot. I was terribly tired, you see…"

Her voice trailed off, but her blue eyes looked both hopeful and perhaps a touch bashful, which surprised and pleased him. They were both aware that she hadn't slept, so he saw the apology for what it was—trying to smooth the awkward moment over. He could be graceful and accept it, or reject it. Considering they had to spend the next week and a half together, rejecting it probably wasn't such a smart idea.

"What brought you around?" He chose to move the conversation along and start over. "When I left you, you looked ready to drop."

He turned his head and looked her square in the face, waiting for her answer. To his surprise she smiled.

"Your coffee. It's very good."

"Kicking Horse. Comes from a place a few hours that way." He thumbed ambiguously toward the west.

"Oh. Well, it's delicious. And I snooped in the pantry

and happened to find a jar of the most delicious cinnamon cookies. Caffeine and sugar have given me my second wind."

"Good to know."

He turned back to his broth, now bubbling on the burner.

"Can I help?"

"You can set the table if you like," he replied, focusing on running a whisk through the gravy, trying not to think about how soft and sweet her voice sounded. "Plates are to the far right of the sink. Glasses one door in."

As she busied herself setting the table, he whisked thickener into the boiling broth. "So, what are you editing, anyway?"

"Just a shoot I did a week or so ago, for a fashion magazine. I'd rather wait to sleep tonight and try to reset my clock—know what I mean? Working keeps me alert."

"You brought work on your vacation?"

She shrugged. "It's hardly a vacation, is it? I'm here to take some pictures for you to use for promotion, right?"

"And take some downtime. Mary said you needed it."

Hope's hands paused on the knives and forks. "What exactly *did* my grandmother say anyway? That's the second time you've mentioned that I 'need' to be here."

Satisfied with the gravy, he poured it into a glass measuring cup which doubled as a low-class gravy boat. Ah, so he'd struck a nerve, if the edge to her voice was anything to go by.

"All she said was that a place like this could do you a world of good. She didn't elaborate."

"'A place like this'?" she repeated, her words slow and deliberate. "This is a rehabilitation ranch for children with injuries and disabilities, isn't it?"

"Yes, it is. And clearly you're not a child. Nor do you have any disabilities that I can see."

He met her gaze then, and something sparked between them. She was about as close to flawless as any woman he'd ever seen. Without her hip-length coat now, and changed into casual jeans and a soft sweater, he could appreciate the long length of her legs and the perky tilt of her breasts beneath the emerald-green material. Her eyes looked the slightest bit tired, but her lips were the perfect balance between being full without being overly generous, and her eyes were the color of bluebells when they bloomed in the pasture in summer. Her silky hair framed a flawless face. Yep—she was beautiful, and his reaction was purely physical.

But he wasn't sure what could be responsible for the reciprocating spark on her end. He certainly wasn't anything to look at. He'd accepted that long ago. In a way he considered his disfigurement part of his penance for being the one left behind after the accident.

The marks were a part of who he was. Take it or leave it. All it took was a look in the mirror to remind him why the ranch and the program were so important. It was all because of Brad and a desperate need to have something good come of their family tragedy. And as Blake had been the one who'd made it out alive, the one who'd been left behind, it was up to him to make it happen.

Her lips thinned as she straightened, her posture was flawless, too. Regal, even. He felt a flicker of admiration.

"I think there's some mistake," she said, her voice clear. "I don't know why on earth my grandmother would have said such a thing, but rest assured, Mr. Nelson. I am perfectly fine and I'm only here because I would walk over broken glass for her."

So he was Mr. Nelson again, and she had made it perfectly clear that she certainly wasn't doing *him* any favors.

"She sounded like she would do anything for you, too."

Blake chafed at her abrasive tone but kept his patience. Tired or not, Hope's pronouncement sounded an awful lot like denial. And he'd put money on it having something to do with her extreme reaction to his face.

"I'll take pictures for you, as she promised on my behalf. But I'm hardly in need of any sort of rehab. In any way. As you can see, I'm perfectly fit."

Oh, she was fit, all right. The way he was noticing the soft curve of her waist and the swell of her breasts beneath the soft sweater was proof enough of that.

"She didn't say it was physical. She led me to believe that it was more…" He was used to talking about these things in a practical manner, so why was it suddenly so difficult with her? So trite and clichéd? "More emotional," he finished. "A different kind of hurt."

Something flickered through her eyes. Fear, vulnerability, pain. Just as quickly it disappeared, but he'd seen it. Her grandmother was right, wasn't she? Hope was doing a fair job of hiding it, but something was causing her pain.

"She's wrong. She hasn't even seen me in over two years," Hope replied coolly, folding her hands. "Sorry. Nothing to fix here."

He shrugged, knowing better than to push right now. "It's okay. I'm just happy to have the pictures for our promo materials. And you never know. Sometimes a few days of R & R can do miraculous things. It doesn't have to be any more complicated than that. I'm just a rancher, Hope. I don't have any interest in prying into your personal life."

Indeed not. He'd been dreading her arrival for days. He might be good at his job but he was hopeless at playing host. Social situations were so not his thing, and as a rule he avoided them as much as possible.

His words did nothing to ameliorate the situation. If

anything they seemed to make it worse. She straightened her shoulders.

"Since that's the case, perhaps it would be best if tomorrow I find another place to stay nearby."

There was an imperious arrogance to her voice that grated on a particular nerve of Blake's. There was being private, and then there was just being uppity, as his father would say. And Hope McKinnon was being uppity. He wondered what it was that put her on the defensive so completely. Clearly she wasn't any happier about being here than he was.

"Suit yourself," he replied smoothly, refusing to take the bait. He had enough to worry about without babysitting a woman who didn't want to be here. At this point as long as he got his pictures he was a happy boy.

He took the platter to the table and put it down in the center. He was very good at being patient. Maybe he was annoyed, but she could issue all sorts of decrees and pronouncements and she wasn't going to fizz him a bit. He'd had tons of practice at hiding his true feelings. Years of it.

Besides, he had more important things to worry about. Like Christmas. And making sure the program kids had some extra good memories to carry them through the holidays. And a sleigh to paint. All of which would keep him out of her way.

Hope sat down at the table and opened a paper napkin, spreading it over her lap like a visiting princess.

As Blake grabbed the carving knife, he set his jaw.

Nothing was going to get in his way. Especially her.

Hope stretched beneath the covers, luxuriating in the soft blankets. The light coming through the window was strange…dim, but somehow bright at the same time. She rubbed the grit from her eyes and checked her watch.

Seven-thirty in the morning. She'd slept for ten hours. Considering the time difference, that was very close to a miracle. She had worked after dinner until she could barely keep her eyes open. That had been the plan. Work. Fall asleep. No time to think.

No time to feel.

She could be very productive this way.

The floor was cold beneath her feet as she tiptoed to the window. Ah, the reason for the odd light was fresh snow. Mounds of it piled up around the barn and fence-posts. Great dollops of it balanced on the branches of the spruce trees in the yard. It looked like a winter fairyland and it kept falling—big, fluffy flakes of it. She felt as if she were looking out on an interactive Christmas card. The kind that landed in her in-box this time of year, with snowmen and Christmas trees to click on.

For a moment it reminded her of home—of Gram's place in Beckett's Run. She imagined Gram would be baking Christmas cookies and getting out the decorations by now. Something that felt like homesickness swept through her as she stared at the snow, so familiar and yet so foreign.

In New England they'd always hoped for a white Christmas. She and her sisters had put on hats and mittens and boots and made snowmen and had snowball fights. Grace had accused Hope of being too bossy about where to put Frosty's nose and Faith could no longer play peacemaker.

Hope smiled to herself. Poor Faith. Hope and Grace hadn't made things easy on their middle sister. Things were slightly better with their relationship now, in so far as Faith wasn't *not* speaking to Hope. Grace was still put out with Hope for not agreeing to go on an assignment with her. In Hope's defense, the opportunity to do a shoot for *Style-Setter* magazine was too good to pass up, but Grace hadn't understood.

Now Faith was in a similar predicament to Hope—Gram had asked a favor of her, too, and she was doing some special stained glass project for an English earl.

Sometimes it seemed like the three of them were on different planets.

A movement to the right caught her attention. It was Blake, bundled in a heavy coat with a black knitted cap on his head and huge gloves on his hands, shoveling the walkway that ran from house to barnyard. Snow flew off his shovel in great puffs as Hope took the time to study him more carefully.

He'd annoyed her with his assessment last night, making her react when she'd truly wanted to be pleasant after getting off on the wrong foot. And in his words he was no therapist. Just a rancher.

Looking at his scar, though, she knew he wasn't any ordinary rancher. This was personal for him, wasn't it? Someone didn't run a place like this without a history. She'd bet it was all wrapped up in how he'd got that scar.

And just like that she knew it would be best if she did move lodgings. What good would come of any sort of curiosity? She didn't want to get caught up in anyone else's drama. She'd had enough of her own to last a lifetime. She had a good life now and she'd fought hard for it, worked hard. Gram was wrong. She didn't need fixing at all. What she needed was to keep busy.

She wished she could snap her fingers and it would be Christmas already. She'd spend it with Gram and then head back to Sydney, where she belonged. She'd rather just forgo all this nonsense altogether.

Hope showered and dried her hair, then got dressed, did her makeup carefully and straightened her unruly curls with a flatiron until they lay soft and smooth to her shoulders. When she finally went downstairs Blake was inside, curling his hands around a coffee cup while steam rose in wisps in the air.

"Good morning."

He turned and smiled as if the tension of last night had never existed. It appeared they were both making an effort.

"Morning."

"Is there more of that?"

He moved his head, gesturing to the coffeemaker. "Help yourself. How'd you sleep?"

She reached for a cup. "Better than I expected. Maybe it's the mountain air. Or going without sleep for nearly forty-eight hours. I slept right through."

"It was still dark after sunrise, thanks to the storm. We really got dumped on overnight. I figured we would."

She poured the coffee and took the first sip—*ah*. The restorative, caffeine-injected brew suddenly seemed to make everything a little more right in the world.

"How much came down?"

"Maybe a foot and a half, and it's still falling."

Her bubble of happiness popped and the coffee didn't taste quite so good. "A foot and a half? Like, eighteen inches?"

"Yeah. Afraid the roads are closed from here to the highway unless you've got a four-by-four. And of course there's always the problem of trying to realize where the road ends and the fields begin. Try it and you're in a ditch and calling a neighbor to haul you out. No one's going anywhere today."

And there it was. Her brilliant plan to be friendly but

insist on going to nearby Banff to find a hotel room blown out of the water. "For how long?" she asked.

"Oh, rest of today for sure. If it lets up things'll be clear by tomorrow sometime. Added to what we already had, there's no doubt it'll be a white Christmas this year."

He grinned with satisfaction—only the second time she'd seen him smile. It seemed the gruff rancher had a soft spot for the holidays. Good for him.

Well, there was nothing to be done about it now. She could manage one more night. She could make some calls today and book a room. She let out a breath.

"You should have some breakfast. I ate early, but Anna's here. She'll fix you up. Anna?"

"You called?"

A raspy voice came from the hall and a woman appeared just after it. She was small—barely over five feet—with eyes black as night and golden-brown skin. "Hope, meet Anna Bearspaw."

The woman smiled, making the skin around her eyes wrinkle, and now Hope understood why her question about whether Anna was his wife or girlfriend had made him laugh. The woman was easily fifty, her graying black hair pulled back in a sleek low ponytail.

"Hope." She grinned. "Blake says you liked my elk last night."

"Elk?" she struggled to keep the pleasant smile pasted on her face. She'd assumed the flavorful meat was beef. Didn't Alberta boast about its beef?

"The roast," Blake offered. "No one does it up like Anna."

Hope had to swallow the saliva that pooled in her mouth at the thought of eating what had to be hunted game. She rarely ate red meat, but had made an exception rather than rock the hospitality boat. She was used to meat coming in neatly wrapped packages at the market. Her stomach turned as she imagined the process of getting a wild animal to the table.

"It was…uh…delicious," she offered weakly.

"My boy John's the hunter. We kept some for ourselves and gave the rest to Blake in trade."

"Trade?"

"It's nothing," Blake said, putting his cup in the sink.

"Oh, it's *nothing*," Anna parroted. She looked at Hope. "Blake has given me a job, and now that it's just me and John at home he looks after us, whatever we need. He's a good man."

It made no sense to Hope why she'd be curious to know more about Anna, but she found herself asking, "Looks after you?"

The woman beamed. "He's a good neighbor."

"We all look after each other out here, that's all," Blake replied.

That was just the sort of thing Hope tried to avoid. She didn't like having to rely on other people. She'd rather rely on her own two hands and abilities. She liked being independent. She liked her job and her circle of friends in Sydney. She had life just the way she wanted it, didn't she? And it was a good life. Relying on help meant people thought they had the right to pry into personal matters. She much preferred privacy.

It hadn't always been that way, though. Not when she'd been a child. Once upon a time the three sisters had stuck together. After their parents had finally split for good they'd had to—they'd only had each other. And Gram.

It had been Gram who had told her to stop trying so hard to hold them all together. And Gram who had witnessed her complete breakdown at eighteen, when stress had meant she'd blown her exams and lost her scholarship. It had been Gram who had picked her up and helped her get back on her feet again. No one but the two of them knew how much it had cost Gram. And Hope had paid back every cent. She'd made sure of that.

She was still working on paying back the personal cost to her grandmother—which was why she'd agreed to this stupid scheme in the first place.

She pushed the painful memories aside and tried to smile for Anna. "If the roads are closed, how did you get here this morning?" She was almost afraid to know the answer. Wondered if she'd look outside and see a dogsled. This all seemed so surreal it didn't feel out of the realm of possibility.

"My snowmobile."

"Of course," she said faintly, quite sure now that she'd ended up in a parallel universe.

"We won't have any clients today. But the snow's supposed to stop, and I've got to scout out a Christmas tree. You can come if you want—see more of the ranch. You could probably use the fresh air after being cooped up in a plane for the better part of two days."

Hope looked over at Blake. He was leaning, completely relaxed, against the kitchen counter. With Anna on one side and Blake's long legs blocking the escape to the hall Hope felt utterly trapped.

"I thought I was supposed to be taking pictures," she replied, scrambling for an excuse. There was no way she was going to straddle a snowmobile and wrap her arms around Blake.

"Bring your camera. I'll take you up to the top of the ridge. The view from there is phenomenal. Mountains as far as you can see. They'll be pretty now with the new snow."

"I don't do landscapes," she explained desperately.

The two of them? Alone in the wilderness? Briefly it struck her how many shoots she'd been on with complete strangers. This was no big deal.

Only it was. Because this didn't feel exactly business-like. And it was impossible it could be anything else. They didn't even like each other, did they?

"A picture's a picture, right?

He was undeterred, and she was feeling more irritated the longer the conversation went on. Anna proceeded to unload the dishwasher as if they weren't even there. A picture was only a picture if you were an amateur. She kept away from nature photographs because she preferred to have control. Her photos were carefully set up, lighting adjusted, models just so. If there were variables *she* wanted to control them.

But she wasn't about to explain that to Blake any more than she'd try to tell him how to do his job. He'd probably find it supernaturally boring. Not many people understood her quest for perfection. Truthfully, she wasn't sure she'd ever find it, but she still kept trying. It was a constant challenge and one she thrived on. Some days that challenge was what got her up in the morning. The possibility of perfection, out there waiting for her to make it happen. Something no one could ever take away from her.

"I don't think I have the right clothing." She tried for a final excuse, knowing this would surely get her out of it. She'd research some hotels instead and book a room, so she could be gone once the roads were cleared. And she'd explain her reasons so he understood. Gram was just trying to look after her, but she was doing just fine looking after herself. She didn't need to impose on his "Western hospitality" for the whole ten days.

"I think we've got gear that'll fit you," he said. "Any more excuses?" He lifted an eyebrow in challenge. "You're not afraid of a snowmobile, are you?"

She really couldn't come up with anything else. She thought about having to climb on the back of the snowmobile, wrapping her arms around his middle. She swallowed. She'd die before explaining about the whole physical proximity thing. It wasn't that she was shy. It was more…

She looked into his face. His eyes were focused on her in a way that made her heart flutter unexpectedly. This was the problem. In the small bit of time since her arrival there'd been an awareness she hadn't either expected or wanted. The angry scar on his face added a sense of danger, and she tried to ignore it as best she could—and the dark feelings it evoked. But his size alone practically screamed masculinity and she wasn't completely immune to that. It was the way he looked at her, the husky but firm tone of his voice that set her nerve endings on edge.

Blake Nelson, for all his broodiness and imperfections, was exciting. It was the last thing she'd expected and it totally threw her off guard.

And now he'd issued a challenge.

She could do this. Besides, after two days of stale recirculated air on the plane she could use the crisp bite of the wind in her face, right?

"I'm game. I guess," she added. He didn't need to know he'd tapped into her competitive streak.

"I'm going to finish up a few things in the barn, so I'll be back in about an hour, okay? Anna knows where the winter gear is. She'll help you."

"Sure I will," the woman answered from behind Hope.

Hope smiled weakly. Well, if nothing else the ride with

Blake would give her the chance to talk to him about switching accommodation.

That was one argument she wouldn't lose.

CHAPTER THREE

BLAKE handed over the helmet and watched as Hope put it on. He hid a smile, wondering if she was worried about messing her perfect hair. "Put down the visor when we start out. It'll keep the wind and snow off your face," he suggested, straddling the padded seat of the snowmobile.

Anna had bundled Hope up in borrowed winter boots, ski pants and jacket, and a thick pair of gloves. She looked different. Approachable. He was enjoying seeing her out of her comfort zone. After last night, with her reading glasses on like armor and her laptop flashed up, he got the sense that her work was her shield.

"Hop on," he called, starting the machine, letting it idle for a few minutes. She slid on behind him, her legs cushioning his. He swallowed and for the first time wondered about the wisdom of the idea of disappearing into the foothills with her.

Then she slid her arms around his ribs.

Even through the thick material of their jackets the contact rippled through him. He scowled and set his teeth, rejecting the surprising whip of arousal. What was the point of being attracted to her? A woman like Hope would never be interested in a man like him. They never were. He and Hope came from different places. He kept his life simple, without frills and fancies. And she was a city girl through and through. A modern woman, independent and successful—not that there was a thing wrong with that.

But nothing good would come of the two worlds colliding.

He hit the throttle. "Hold on!" he called, and gave it a shot of gas, taking them up and over a snowbank before heading over the snowy field to the crest beyond.

The zipper of her jacket seemed to dig into his back but he ignored it as they cruised over the undulating hills. The snow had stopped, only the odd errant flake drifting lazily down now to settle gently atop the pristine white blanket covering the meadow. In the summertime he wandered these hills on horseback to calm his mind. But in winter he used one of the snowmobiles that Anna kept at her place for her and John.

He reached the crest of the ridge and slowed, coming to a stop by an outcropping of rock that sat oddly out of place in the middle of the land. He cut the engine, dismounting. It was his favorite place on the ranch when all was said and done.

It was where he and Brad had come as boys. Identical twins, they'd done everything together. They'd made campfires and built a hooch in the shade of the rock, unrolling sleeping bags and spending the night with nature. They'd talked about hockey, talked about playing in the NHL someday, talked about the farm and, as they got a little older, girls.

Now Blake usually came alone. Sometimes to remember. Sometimes to look down at the awesome view—the way the land dipped and then extended straight out to the mountains—and to realize that he was just one small part of the big world out there. It helped him put things in perspective after a bad day.

He'd been surprised at himself for issuing the invitation

to Hope. Perhaps it was that little glimpse of vulnerability that had prompted him to do it. And the knowledge that he felt the need for the wind on his face and it wouldn't be very hospitable to take off and leave her stranded at the house alone.

Maybe he wasn't entirely pleased with the houseguest arrangement, but he liked to think his parents had taught him decent manners.

"This is nice," Hope said, climbing off the snowmobile and peeling the helmet off her head. Her hair was matted down beneath a thin toque and she pulled the hat straight. Pieces of blond hair stuck out like straw around her ears.

"Nice?" he repeated, somehow deflated by her bland reaction to the spectacular panorama before them. He breathed deeply, watched as his breath formed a frosty cloud that disappeared. "It's kind of a miracle, don't you think? That places like this exist?"

"I suppose," she answered, taking a few steps through the snow toward him. "It certainly is a big view."

He turned his head to study her. "The best adjectives you can come up with are 'nice' and 'big'?"

She smiled then. "So my attempts to downplay it are a major fail?" She shrugged, then took a deep breath and let it out. "Okay, you win. I admit it. It's stunning up here."

"That's better." He nodded and went to the biggest rock, used his arm to dust the snow off its surface. "Care to sit, Your Highness?"

He offered her his hand but she ignored his gesture, climbed up nimbly and perched on the rock, drawing up her knees and looking out over the landscape. "What is this place, anyway?"

"The outer edge of the ranch property. We used to own more, but I sold a chunk of it off years ago."

"Why?"

He was a little startled at her question, especially as she'd shown very little interest in the ranch side of things since her arrival. "I didn't need as much grazing land once I sold off the cattle. I just needed enough for the horses and feed."

"You had cattle?"

"My family did, yes."

"Why did you sell them off?" She was quiet for a moment but he knew she wanted to ask something more. Finally she looked over at him. "Was the ranch in trouble?"

He shook his head. "No. But when my dad decided to go into early retirement after a heart attack scare the ranch was left in my hands. It was up to me to make the decisions. This is what I chose." He shrugged. "The therapy part and the funding I receive covers the operational expenses. The horses I board give me something to live on."

And it hadn't been easy either. Despite being in charge, he had wanted his parents' support. His father had thought he was crazy when he'd broached the idea of selling off the majority of the ranch to fund a rehabilitation program. Once the assets of land and cattle were gone they were gone for good. But when he'd explained about how difficult it had been, growing up with not only the scarring but the lingering effects of the accident, about how he needed to do something worthwhile, they'd come around. Now his parents helped out during the spring and summer. In some ways this program was a living memorial to Brad.

"Where are your parents now?"

"Phoenix. They're snowbirds. They have a condo down there and avoid the cold Canadian winters. They'll be back for Christmas though, flying in Christmas Eve. Mom always says it doesn't feel like Christmas without snow."

Hope didn't answer, and Blake studied her profile. She was tanned from living in Sydney, her blond hair streaked from the sun. She turned her head and looked at him and he realized the combination made her eyes stand out. Right now, in the cold crisp air, they were the precise color of a mountain bluebird.

"What about you? What are you doing for Christmas?"

She shrugged, but he thought he saw a shadow pass over the brightness of her eyes. "I'll fly out of here to Boston, and then on to Beckett's Run to spend the holidays with my grandmother. And I suppose any other members of my family who might show up."

"You're all spread out, then?"

She rubbed her hands together as if they were cold. "So what made you switch from cattle producer to equine therapy?"

She was changing the subject. Clearly her family was a sore spot with her. Was that the problem that her grandmother had mentioned? He reminded himself that it was none of his concern, but found he was curious anyway. Were they estranged?

But she'd turned the tables and asked a question and he knew she expected an answer. He pointed at his scar. "This."

She looked away.

"I know it's bad," he said. "I see it every day."

"It's not that bad," she said quietly, but she looped her arms around her knees, shutting him out. "I've seen worse."

Those three words seemed to explain a lot and nothing all at once. "But it does make you uncomfortable?"

She looked at him. "I suppose that makes me a bad person?"

She was so defensive. He let out a breath. "Depends. Depends on why, right? Someone like you—you're used to dealing with beautiful models all day long. You're probably not used to—"

He broke off. He refused to refer to himself as ugly. He'd spent too long digging himself out of his hole of grief to allow negative thinking.

"Now who's judging and making assumptions?"

It bugged him that she was right.

She looked him square in the face—not to the side, not over his shoulder—dead in his eyes.

"If it makes me uncomfortable it's not for the reasons you think. I just… It just reminds me of someone, that's all."

"And remembering hurts?"

She looked back out over the fields, but he saw a muscle tick in her jaw. "Yeah. I guess it does. So I try not to. It's easier that way."

He could relate to that more than she'd ever know. Instead of answering he let the quiet of the winter day work its magic. He sat on the rock beside her—far enough away that they weren't touching—and listened. To the wind shushing through the stand of spruce trees nearby. To the faint sound of the sparse flakes of snow touching the ground. No traffic. No nothing. Just space.

"How did it happen?" she finally asked.

He'd explained it many times, but each time his throat clogged up a little. The memory never dimmed. It was never less horrific, even after all this time.

"We were coming home from a hockey tournament in British Columbia. We had an accident."

"You played hockey?"

He tried to smile. "Still do—a little pond hockey. You'll see. Some of the neighborhood teenagers come over and have a go at it. I'll have to clean the rink off tomorrow. It's covered in snow now."

"You're a real kid person, aren't you?"

"I suppose I am." He aimed a level look at her. "Kids are great. Full of energy and curiosity."

"Loud, destructive, unpredictable…"

She was smiling a little now. She looked awfully pretty when she smiled like that.

He cleared his throat, uncomfortable at her observation. He liked to keep his personal life personal. It was easier to talk about the ranch and his program than it was to talk about himself.

"Perhaps. But they're also generally accepting." At least the younger kids. Older ones could be cruel—his high school experience could attest to that—but the teens around here had known Blake long enough that his face was no big deal.

"The way most adults aren't?" Her smile slipped. "I suppose it has something to do with loss of innocence. It makes us grown-ups a bit jaded after a while."

Damn, but she had a knack of saying a lot without revealing much of anything. He kind of admired that. "I take it you're not much of a kid person?"

"I don't think I've actually thought about it much."

"You've been too busy searching for the perfect picture?" Burying herself in work, if he could venture a guess. He got the feeling that Hope McKinnon was a pro at losing herself in her job. They had that in common, then.

Her lips twitched. "Something like that. It's not something I'd want to do on my own, if ever. I'm only thirty. I haven't really thought much about the whole marriage and kids thing."

There was something about the way her gaze slid from his that made him think she was lying. "Building your career, I suppose?"

She brightened. "Of course. I love what I do, and with

all the long hours and the travel it's not really conducive to husbands or kids. Anyway, I still have time, right?"

Her smile was bright—possibly too bright.

"I don't know." He shrugged. "How much time do any of us really have?"

"You're a great one for philosophical questions, Blake."

"I have a tendency to overthink."

She put a hand over her mouth in feigned surprise, then dropped it to her lap. "A fault? Surely not? I was starting to think you didn't have any."

"How could you possibly know in less than twenty-four hours?"

"Oh, I'm a quick study. Occupational hazard. And you're an easy read."

Something inside him started to warm as he realized with some surprise that they were bantering. Was she flirting? Hard—no, impossible—to believe. "Are you teasing me?"

"I am. You're awfully serious."

"That's what I thought about you."

She shook her head. "No. I'm focused. Big difference. I know I probably seemed serious yesterday, but really I do know how to have fun. I know how to relax. Who wants to walk around stressed all the time? I like my job, my apartment, my social life. No worries and all that."

They were silent again for a few minutes, but then Blake had to ask the question that was burning in his mind. "If that's true, then why does it seem you carry the weight of the world on your shoulders?"

And there it was. That flash of vulnerability. Just for a moment, but there all the same. Hope might put on a strong, capable show but underneath there was more. A lot more.

And Blake knew that unfortunately he had a soft spot

for birds with broken wings. Seeing as he'd been one once upon a time. He should take her back to the house and keep it strictly business from here on out. But Hope McKinnon was intriguing. The face she showed the world wasn't the real Hope, was it?

Hope hopped down from the rock. "I'm cold. I'm going to walk around a bit and take a few pictures."

He let her go, holding back the observation that she'd said she didn't do landscapes. He watched as she took her camera out from beneath her jacket and moved around, studying angles and light as she snapped. The camera was what had dug into his back on the drive out, he realized. He liked watching her in action. Her face took on a determined set as she focused. But he noticed too that she frowned a lot, a crease forming between her brows. That search for perfection again?

He looked around him at the splendor of the Rockies. It never failed to catch his breath and fill his soul. What could she find to fault in such a magnificent creation?

He hopped down, too, now that the cold of the rock was seeping through his lined pants, making his butt chilly. "What's the matter?" he called, wading through the snow to where she stood, glaring at a particular peak.

"It's not right. The lighting is wrong. With this cloud, that side of the mountain is going to be too shadowed."

"Can't exactly control *that,* right?"

"Exactly. This is why I don't do landscapes and nature shots. There are too many variables. I like to be able to set it up, get the conditions right."

"Yet in all that planning you still haven't found the perfect shot?"

The look she threw in his direction was annoyed. "No. Not yet."

"I think I know the problem," he said, starting to smile. "You're missing the magic."

Her mouth dropped open. "Did you just say *magic?*" She made a sound that was both sarcastic and dismissive. "There's no such thing."

"And that's why you haven't found it. You're a nonbeliever. You can't organize perfection. You can't plan it. It just happens. And when it does, it's magic." Confidence filled his voice.

"You're talking nonsense," she said, shutting her camera off and tucking it back inside her jacket.

She zipped up the coat right to her neck. If she'd been vulnerable before that was all gone now. Instead she was defensive. He supposed she had a right. He did seem to enjoy challenging her, and they barely knew each other.

"I'll bet you that by the end of your time here you'll have your perfect photo, and it won't have a thing to do with planning or staging the scene."

She laughed—a sharp sound in the stillness. "That's an unfair bet. I'd win."

"What if I win? What do I get?"

She stalked back to the snowmobile. "It won't matter anyway. I'll take your pictures, Blake. I'll do promo shots for the ranch and the program. But I think I'd rather stay somewhere else. This is your private home. I don't belong here. I'm going to make some calls and book into a hotel in Banff."

Blake stared at her. He'd really struck a nerve if she couldn't even stand being in the same house as him for a few days. And, while the whole arrangement had been odd from the beginning, he was somehow a little offended that she was so desperate to leave.

Not that she was actually going anywhere. This close to Christmas there wouldn't be a room to spare in the resort town. She was stuck here even if she didn't know it yet. And he wasn't about to be the one to tell her. He doubted Ms. McKinnon liked to be told anything. She could figure it out on her own.

"Can we go back now? I'm getting cold."

"Sure," he answered.

They got back on the snowmobile and he started the engine, revved the throttle and turned them around, heading back to the warmth and comfort of the ranch house.

As they glided over the rolling hills Blake thought about all she'd said, and what she hadn't. If he were a betting man he'd guess that she was a workaholic and she was lonely. Hope was in some serious need of holiday cheer. Problem was, he was the last person able to give it to her.

Hope hit the "end" button on her cell phone and scowled at the display. That was the fifth hotel she'd tried and there were no vacancies anywhere. She didn't even consider calling the Banff Springs—she wasn't hurting for money, but the hundreds of dollars a night price tag was definitely out of her budget for a ten-day stay.

She should have known. Major resort town, so close to the holidays… She was going to be stuck here at Bighorn.

The thought made her stomach turn nervously. Not just because she'd been borderline rude to Blake up at the ridge and now had to make nice. But because on one level she'd actually enjoyed talking to him. She'd let down her guard for a few minutes and had nearly told him about Julie, nearly mentioned her family. For a moment, as she'd stared at the awe-inspiring peaks and snowy valleys, she'd been tempted to confess that the weight on her shoulders, her search for perfection, came from years of trying to make everything right, to create a perfect family that had never existed and never would.

They'd all let her down. Even Julie. Hope had thought
to create her own special family, based on love rather than
genetics. But the result had been the same. At the end of
the day she stood alone. It was time to accept that she just
wasn't good at family.

That she'd wanted to unload all of that on a virtual
stranger hadn't just surprised her—it had been scary. The
last thing she wanted to do was open the Pandora's Box
that was her childhood. It was easier to keep it locked
away and focus on the here and now. The present was all
anyone had control over anyway.

She flopped back on the bed and sighed. She hadn't
been lonely, as such. And she wasn't bitter, just guarded.
Careful. She didn't share secrets or confidences. She
wasn't even close to her sisters anymore. She and Grace
always argued and it wasn't much wonder that Faith had
chosen a calmer path than trying to run interference between them.

It *had* been lonely, she supposed. At times.

Right now she had to even things out with Blake in
order to make the best of the next several days—especially
as she had no place to go.

Problem was there had been a moment today when
he'd looked in her eyes and she'd had the most irrational
impulse to tell him *everything*.

She'd have to watch that.

She put her phone on to charge and decided to wander
downstairs. She could always check the pictures from
today and see if any were salvageable. And she really
needed to talk to Blake about more practical matters—
like what sorts of shots he wanted for his promo materials and how they were going to make that happen. She
needed to think of this as a job. It would make the time
go faster—and easier.

She'd booted up her laptop and inserted her memory card when she heard the back door open and close, followed by a heavy stomping of boots.

Blake came in, his cheeks ruddy from the cold, his eyes glowing even brighter than before. His hair was disheveled from wearing the heavy hat, giving him a boyish, roguish appearance. If it weren't for the jagged gash on the side of his face he'd be gorgeous, she realized. The men she knew paid stylists a fortune to achieve that tumbled, rugged look, and spent hours at the gym to gain a physique that Blake had mastered from simple physical labor on the ranch.

She'd been staring at him far too long. She dropped her gaze back to the computer screen and used the mouse to bring up the day's photos. "You look cold," she remarked blandly.

"The temperature's dropped. Animals are in for the night, though. Snug as a bug."

"That's good," she said, skimming the photos. A few weren't half bad, she realized, though her instincts had been correct—the lighting wasn't right. She might be able to play around with them, but none stood out as anything special or noteworthy.

"Anna's gone?" he asked, rubbing his hands together and going to the sink. He ran water and washed his hands, reaching for a towel hanging on the inside of a cupboard door.

"I think I heard her leave just before it started getting dark. When I came downstairs I checked, and there's what looks to be a lasagna in the oven for dinner."

"Gosh, that sounds good." He hung the towel back up. "I'll throw together a salad and some garlic bread to go with it."

"You're quite the cook."

"Lots of guys cook, you know."

She did know, but she had a hard time picturing Blake in the kitchen. He was so…large and manly. She smiled to herself. Maybe she'd been working in fashion too long. "So why keep a housekeeper if you're so capable?"

He lifted a shoulder. "Anna needs the work. I know how to run a washing machine and the vacuum and kitchen appliances. But it's nice sometimes, especially after a long day, to not have to worry about it. I cook for myself on the weekends. I make a French toast to die for."

She imagined Blake pushing a vacuum over the living room rug, pictured his long fingers wrapped around a spatula, flipping eggy bread. She found the image strangely attractive.

"What's so funny?" he asked.

She looked up and grinned. "I was just picturing you in an apron."

Something odd and strangely exciting seemed to curl through her stomach as she looked up at him. He was so reserved. Not just reserved…guarded. He'd mentioned an accident today but stopped short of giving any real insight. She found herself growing more and more curious about him.

"Blake, about this afternoon…"

At her serious tone he put a loaf of French bread down on the countertop beside her. The breakfast nook and stools were a great place for her to work but she suddenly felt like he was very close and her pulse quickened in response.

"What about it?"

"I think I owe you an apology. Some of your questions made me uncomfortable and I think I came across as rude."

He studied her carefully until she wondered if she was

starting to blush beneath the scrutiny. There was something simmering between them, something she couldn't quite put her finger on, but it felt suspiciously like he could read her mind. She wasn't sure she liked someone poking around in her thoughts.

"No hotel rooms available, eh?"

Heat flashed to her cheeks. She was definitely blushing now. He'd seen clear through her apology, hadn't he? She was totally busted. A bit irritated, too, though—because her remorse was genuine.

"Even if there were," she said quietly, "I was snippy with you and you didn't deserve it."

"Why were you?"

"You always ask the hard questions, don't you?" She put down the cover of her laptop and looked up at him.

"Not hard. Just real."

"From where I'm sitting they're the same thing."

His gaze softened. "I'm used to challenging people, I guess. Pushing to break through what's holding them back."

"I'm not here to be fixed or rehabilitated," she reminded him firmly. He'd been rather cryptic himself, out on the ridge. But she wouldn't bring that up right now. She was trying to smooth things over, not begin another argument. "I just keep to myself, you know? When I said today that your scar reminded me of someone, you asked if it hurt. It does."

"Who was he?"

She paused, surprised that he'd assumed it was a man she was speaking of—though she supposed she shouldn't be. She was thirty years old. Blake probably assumed she'd had relationships before. And she had, though never anything serious.

"Not a he. A she. My best friend. Her name was Julie."

She took a breath, surprised that she'd actually come right out and said it. She never talked about Julie. Her throat tightened but she forced the heavy feeling away, shutting it out.

She swallowed away the pain and forced herself to continue. "We shared everything. Work, interests, TV shows…an apartment."

"What happened?"

"There was a fire at a nightclub." Hope's throat felt like it was going to close over, and she fought to swallow, to keep going without thinking about it all too much. She could say it, offer a basic explanation so they could move on, right? "She was burned very badly. It was the worst thing ever to see her like that. First with all the bandages and then, briefly, without."

"What happened to her?"

Hope blinked, but her eyes were stone-dry. "She died. It was too much for her body to take and she went into organ failure."

She didn't have to say more for them both to understand how it had been a long and painful illness.

"I'm sorry."

She felt grief hover around the edges and began to panic. She had to change the focus. Put it somewhere else. She looked up and saw Blake's scar before her eyes. Painful truth slammed into her heart. "I saw you yesterday…" She heard her voice shake and tried to steady it. "I saw you and it was like seeing her…"

She couldn't finish.

Blake's hand closed over hers, warm and strong. The contact rippled through her, past the wall she usually built around herself, past the wall she sensed he kept around himself, too. Oh, it felt good to be connected to someone again. Terrifying but reassuring all at once.

All too soon he pulled away. It was just as well, she thought, tucking her fingers into her lap. She didn't trust it. Didn't trust the caring, tender gesture. Didn't trust herself to be objective.

"When?"

The simple question took her by surprise. "When what?"

"When did she die?"

Her gaze was drawn to his. There was no judgment in the blue depths, just patience. "About six months ago," she found herself answering.

"You haven't grieved yet."

He was getting too close to the truth. It wasn't any of his business if she had or hadn't. What was the point in indulging in a fit of grief? Crying and self-pity wouldn't bring Julie back and it wouldn't fix anything—another lesson learned the hard way at too young an age.

If only tears had the power to make things right life would have been so different. For all of them. She and her sisters wouldn't have been dragged from pillar to post. There wouldn't have been the arguments that Hope had always heard, even through walls. There wouldn't have been the crying for Daddy in bed at night with the covers over her head. She would have been able to hold them together. They would have been one big happy family instead of the mess they became.

"Of course I have," she lied, more shaken than she cared to admit.

"Grief can be crippling in itself," he explained. "At some point you have to deal with it."

She was starting to get angry now. How dared he talk to her like he had her all figured out? He knew nothing about her.

She took a slow, deep breath and held her temper. Losing it wouldn't do either of them any good. Instead she tried a smile that felt stretched and artificial. "Look, I just didn't want you to think it's…well, that it's you. Or that I'm…" She found she couldn't go on, couldn't say the word that had flashed into her brain. *Superficial.* The words trailed away.

"That you're prejudiced?"

Her gaze clashed with his. "Why would I think less of someone because of a scar?"

"I don't know. It makes me wonder if you look for perfection in people like you do in your pictures."

"People aren't perfect. Everyone knows that."

His lips curved up a little bit. "I agree. And apology accepted. Let's eat."

She felt utterly off balance as Blake let the topic drop and shifted gears into dinner mode. She put the photos away and went to help him with the garlic bread and salad. The sound of the evening news on the television provided a welcome chatter in the silence. But as she set the table his words echoed uncomfortably in her mind. *Did* she expect people to be perfect? Or was it knowing they weren't that made her keep everyone at arm's length?

CHAPTER FOUR

THE snowplows had been and the roads were open the next day. The ranch yard was a hub of activity by midmorning. There were extra cars in the driveway. Blake had had the chores done before Hope was even out of bed, and she'd eaten breakfast alone in the kitchen—Anna had the day off to do Christmas shopping in Calgary.

Hope looped her camera strap around her neck before putting on her puffy red jacket. It looked cold, so she put mittens on her hands—the kind with flaps that flipped up to leave her fingers exposed—and a knitted hat with a small funky peak on top of her head. Maybe she needed to be warm, but that didn't mean she had to be styleless. It had been a while since she'd put up with a northern winter but she did know how.

And after last night, and the confidences she'd shared with Blake, she felt the need to hit a reset button. It would be better to keep things businesslike from here on in, right? Professional. She was here to take pictures, and that was exactly what she was going to do.

The barn was warmer than she'd expected, considering the frosty bite to the air outside. Voices came from the riding ring and she made her way in that direction, taking in the scent of horse and hay as she walked down the corridor. It was a pleasant scent, and reminded her of early adolescence when, typical for her age, she'd gone through a horse stage and wanted her own. The answer had always been no, though eventually she'd worn her parents down and they'd agreed to riding lessons.

She'd had exactly three wonderful lessons when Mom had left Dad—again—and they'd moved.

She sighed. And people wondered why she didn't let herself count on anyone—or anything—too much. Her parents' marriage hadn't been an easy one. Whoever said opposites attract was dead wrong. It was a recipe for disaster. Her mom and dad hadn't balanced each other out. They'd driven each other crazy—Lydia with her flighty ways and Greg always trying to clip her wings. Hope had felt left in the gap—a child herself, but with the responsibility of raising her sisters. She hadn't done a very good job.

She stopped and took a few pictures of the long corridor of stalls. The floor was neat as a pin, and the inside of the tack room was exactly the same—saddles lined up precisely, bridles hung on thick pegs, a stack of heavy blankets a splash of color in a room that was decidedly brown. She liked it, actually, the leather and wood were rich and redolent with character and a certain Western charm.

She experimented with a few different angles and adjustments for several minutes, losing herself in the task. Finally, when she was satisfied, she made her way to the entrance to the riding ring.

The first thing to catch her eye was Blake. He stood in the middle of the ring, boots planted a few feet apart and his hands on his hips. He wore a red long-sleeved shirt with a puffed black vest over the top and a cowboy hat on his head. Her gaze traveled up his long legs to the worn pockets of his jeans and her lips went dry.

On impulse she lifted her camera, turned it to capture

him from top to bottom. She zoomed in so that his tall figure filled the viewfinder. There was no posing, no setting the scene, but right now he didn't need it. Besides, this wasn't an official photo for the site or anything. She'd work with him on that, so he'd have some sort of head shot he could use for promotion. This, she admitted to herself, was purely self-indulgent. A whim. She'd probably end up hitting the "delete" key in the end anyway.

Two horses with riders slowly circled the ring, and Hope watched as the first rider—a girl of perhaps ten— looked at Blake and smiled widely. He called out some encouragement, and then something else to the next rider—a boy who looked to be a similar age. As Hope watched the girl stopped her horse and stayed to the side, while the boy trotted up to Blake, turned and trotted back to his first position. Then it was the girl's turn.

It wasn't until Hope took a moment to take a full look around the perimeter of the ring that she saw two women, probably the moms, standing to one side, smiling and chatting.

There was too much activity right now to get the pictures she wanted. She'd rather the ring was empty. In her mind she analyzed the different views and vantage points, the available natural light and what fixtures were installed within the building. Wouldn't it be neat to be able to get a bird's-eye view of the ring? But she had no idea how she'd get up to the rafters to take it. She'd done some daring things to get a shot before, but suspending herself from a ceiling was one she hadn't tried yet.

The lesson ended and the boy and girl dismounted and began leading their horses to the exit. Hope slid aside, pressing herself to the wall to give them lots of room as they passed. She tilted her head as she watched them go by. They didn't look disabled in any way. They looked like a normal boy and girl.

Blake was right on their heels and he gave her a brief nod, but that was all. She hung back and watched as he efficiently cross-tied the animals in the corridor. The kids, barely five feet tall, began the process of removing the tack. Blake stepped forward and helped take the weight of the saddle from each of them. But the rest he let them do alone.

He came over to her then, keeping an eye on the children the whole time. "Hey," he said. "Wondered if you were ever going to get up."

"My days and nights are still a little messed up," she commented. "You were out here already when I dragged my sorry butt out of bed. It was a pretty cozy nest I had going on."

His gaze fell on her and she tried to ignore the warm buzz of awareness that ran through her.

"They do all that themselves?" she asked.

He grinned easily and she realized he was quite different out here in his element. More relaxed, less of a chip on his shoulder. He moved his attention from her and nodded in the direction of the children. "They do now. Not at first, though. Both Jennie and Riley are autistic. It took quite some time for us to get them to this point."

"I wondered. They look like normal kids."

He frowned. "They *are* normal kids."

Oh, she'd hit a nerve, she realized. Quite unintentionally, but she probably should have chosen her words better. "What I meant to say is they don't have a visible disability."

"I know what you meant. It's a bit of a battle, though. Drawing the line between normal and abnormal is what can make it so hard for these kids, you know? It really shouldn't matter what challenges they have. They have feelings like anyone else."

There was a sharpness to his tone that made her look up. The line of his jaw was firm and, if her guess was right, defensive. "Of course they do. I never meant to imply otherwise."

"I find it hard to take off my crusader's hat at times."

She wondered if that was because at one time he had been one of those kids. Had he been teased, picked on? Had there been more to his injury than facial deformity? She wasn't any stranger to that either. She'd been a head taller than every other kid in her class from an early age. The names "Beanpole" and "Spider Legs" had hung on for years. Her prom date had been two inches shorter than her, and she'd worn plain flats when all her friends had on heels. Her own father had called her Stringbean.

It was a far cry from a disability, but the teasing had hurt just the same, making her sensitive to the situation of both Blake and his clients. Even now she had to remind herself to stand up straight, rather than slump in an attempt to conceal her height.

"Don't apologize for being passionate about what you do. You're clearly good at it," she said gently.

She bit back her questions about why he'd become that crusader. Even if she did want to know more about him, now was not the time or place. Any answer she got would be short and unsatisfactory.

He leaned against the wall and folded his arms, watching as the little girl returned from the tack room with a bucket of brushes and began grooming her mount.

"Why don't you tell me a little about them?"

The question seemed to satisfy him, and the harsh expression melted away as he watched the duo closely.

"Well," he said, affection warming his voice, "take

Jennie, there. I put her on Minstrel and Riley on Pokey from the beginning, because the gelding and mare are gentle and work well together. That's important when there's more than one rider involved. We couldn't actually put them together at first. It took a lot of work. But they have similar issues and are a similar age. By pairing them up it's not just the two horses that work well with the riders, but the riders work together, too."

"They clearly like you," she added. Blake was quite easy to like, after all—at least in this setting. Easier than she was comfortable with. "The way Jennie smiled at you out there…"

"She's something, isn't she?" He grinned as he watched the youngsters work. "At the beginning she nearly froze in the saddle and didn't say a word. I had to walk Minstrel around the ring while her mom stayed alongside. Finally she started taking the reins herself, but her mom was always right there. Now Heather watches from the sidelines. Seeing Jennie that comfortable and confident—well, that's what this program is all about."

His easy speech took Hope by surprise. In the two days she'd been here he hadn't ever said so much, and so freely. "Is it always just you? It must be a lot of work running this by yourself."

"Oh, no. Jennie and Riley are at a point now where I don't need extra staff or therapists for their sessions. We have to look at the individual child's needs. Safety is the first priority."

Hope looked up at Blake again, examined the dark scar running down his face. Julie had needed someone like Blake. Julie—who'd cried pitifully and without tears when she'd realized her career was over. When she'd understood that she'd never be beautiful again. Hope's throat swelled and she found it hard to swallow. Julie had realized that she'd never get married, have children, be a grandmother. Seeing a person's face when they understood they were going to die was a terrible, terrible thing.

She turned her attention to Riley for a moment as she pulled herself together. He wasn't smiling, and his tongue was between his teeth as he ran a brush over Pokey's hide. "Riley looks tense."

"Riley's very precise. He likes things a certain way, and it's easy for him to get overwhelmed. Riding's only part of it. Right now they're grooming. Once they put the horses back in their stalls they'll make sure they have fresh water and a little treat."

"Really?"

He nodded. "Jennie and Riley both have autism but they're very highly functioning. It works putting them together because they both get overwhelmed and stressed very easily, and frustrated when they can't communicate. Riding is soothing—the gait is very rhythmic and calming—and working with the horses is tactile. And by having to care for them they are practicing making connections, you know? That's so important."

"Mister Blake!" Riley came running up. "Mom brought carrots for Pokey."

Blake smiled at the boy and nodded. "When he's brushed, you can give him one."

Riley looked over at Jennie. "Maybe Jennie would like one for Mist...Mist..."

"For Minstrel? Why don't you ask her?"

They watched curiously as Riley hesitantly approached Jennie.

Jennie nodded at Riley, her ponytail flopping, and Blake smiled. "I'll be..." he murmured. "They don't talk to each other much. Mostly to the horses. It's a big thing that Riley went to her just now. Look."

Riley's mom gave him two carrots, and he promptly took one to Jennie. "Not 'til they're all brushed," Riley instructed.

Jennie nodded solemnly and tucked the treat into her jacket. Blake laughed as Minstrel nudged at Jennie's pocket. "Not yet," she chided the horse. "Soon."

"You're not taking any pictures," he noted, keeping an eye on the kids but confident things were well in hand.

Truth be told Hope had forgotten about her camera. Her interest had been captured by the workings of the place and talking to Blake. "I got a few of the barn while you were in the ring."

He wrinkled his brow. "None of the session? There's no problem with having our kids in the photos."

She looked past him when she answered. "If you're going to use the pictures for promotion you'd have to get all the parents to sign a release. This way is just easier."

Jennie came over. "I'm done. Can I put Minstrel in his stall now?"

Blake laughed. "That carrot burning a hole in your pocket?"

Jennie looked puzzled as she took his joke literally and didn't understand, so he turned to Hope. "Hope, this is Jennie. Jennie, this is Hope. Hope takes pictures, Jennie. She's going to take pictures of the ranch for me."

Hope said a quiet "Hi," but Jennie's smile faded and she seemed to withdraw.

"It's okay," he said to Hope as Jennie turned and trotted back to Minstrel. "She finds meeting new people daunting. That she even came over while you were standing here is progress. She hardly talked when she started."

"How do you know all this stuff?" Hope asked, looking up at him curiously.

"I had to be certified through the Canadian Therapeutic

Riding Association. That's the national board that governs everything. Anyway, we're still pretty small here, and this time of year isn't as busy—especially the few weeks leading up to Christmas. Spring and summer, when the weather turns nicer, it really books up. We do outdoor trail rides then, and other activities rather than just using the ring—including summer camps. I have some volunteers who come in to help, and some of our kids have medical teams that we work closely with—like physios or occupational therapists. This afternoon you'll meet Cate Zerega. Completely different situation than Jennie and Riley."

"How so?"

He kept one eye on the kids' progress as he answered. "She's got cerebral palsy and she's in a wheelchair. It's a lot to deal with when you're six."

Riley was having trouble getting Pokey unclipped so Blake stepped forward. "I'll be back in a bit," he said, leaving Hope standing there alone.

She watched as he smiled at Riley and soothed the boy's nerves. Together they unclipped the horse, and Riley put him in his stall without further incident. It was then that the carrots came out, and Blake laughed as he showed them how to hold out their hands flat. Jennie giggled as her horse's fuzzy nose touched her hand. Blake spoke for a few minutes with the mothers.

Hope had been thinking a lot about what Blake had said last night about her expecting people to be perfect. She wasn't quite sure what to make of it. She liked things a certain way. Didn't everyone? But it had made her think about growing up, and how many times she'd wished her parents had been different—wished they'd stop fighting, stop getting on and off the merry-go-round of their marriage.

That was what had kept her awake late into the night last night. She'd remembered how for a while things would be good, but then the arguing would start again, and then Dad would have had enough, and Mom would decide to take the girls on a new adventure. It hadn't always felt very adventurous. Hope and her sisters had had little stability through those years. Gram had been it.

Hope had tried her best for her sisters. She'd tried to hold it all together by getting perfect grades and trying to fill the gaps that their mother had left in her wake. She'd always felt like a failure, though. Every time Grace got in trouble or Faith got tears in her eyes from having her feelings hurt. Hope, being the oldest, had always felt she understood more about what was happening than the other two. Faith, the tenderhearted one, and Grace, the defensive one. It had been Hope who'd had to step in to dry tears or fix what was broken. Hope who had made sure everyone had a packed lunch and their homework completed.

And now the sisters hardly spoke. How was it she had messed it all up despite trying so hard, and Blake seemed to manage to put pieces back together so naturally?

A more grounded man she'd never met. He seemed comfortable in any situation, didn't he? He had his place in the world and was secure in it. It was evident in his business, his house, the way he grabbed a dish towel and washed dishes or shoveled a walk. This was his corner of the world. And, while Hope loved her life in Sydney, she'd never quite called it home. Home was Beckett's Run, and even then it had never had the permanence that she craved.

She turned away from the cozy scene with the kids and bit her lip. She'd been here two whole days and already it was bringing back things she didn't like to think about. What was the use of dredging up past mistakes? She couldn't change the past. And the truth was she couldn't make everyone fit into the ordered existence she wanted—

she *needed*. They'd all left her anyway. Every single one. She'd given up trying so she could save her own sanity.

It was time she got out of her own head and back to work. She went back into the ring and walked around the edge, snapping different angles. If she could get a good picture of the barn—despite the snow—and a long shot of the stable area, she could probably put together a good spread featuring the main facilities. It wasn't exactly art, but that wasn't what Blake was looking for, was it?

He found her standing in the middle of the dirt floor, much in the same way she'd found him standing only an hour before. "Hey."

She turned and watched him stride across the loam, his long legs eating up the distance. He moved purposefully, with a loose-hipped grace that was sexy as all get out. His cowboy hat shadowed his face, but she could see his lips were set. Her fingers tightened around the camera and without thinking twice she began snapping —rapid shots, one after the other.

"What are you doing in here?"

"Trying some things out. Do you think I could get up there somehow? It'd be cool to get a bird's-eye view of the ring from above."

His eyes opened wide and there was a long pause. Then, "I could get a block and tackle," he mused, rubbing his hand along his chin.

"Really?" She stared up at the beams and then heard his low chuckle. He was making fun of her. "Ha, ha."

"You took off before you could meet the moms."

"I didn't realize you wanted me to."

He frowned. "I wanted you to talk to them about including Riley and Jennie in your pictures. They'll be back next week for the Christmas party. You could get shots then, I suppose. But we won't have a regular session with them again while you're here. You missed the opportunity."

"I didn't know you were serious about that." She looked up at him and felt a little spiral of guilt as she offered the teensy white lie. "I thought it would just be easier if I took pictures of the rig empty."

"Shouldn't your pictures include what we *do,* not just where we do it?"

She bit her lip, unwilling to confess that she'd had to escape the corridor because she'd gotten emotional. "But those pictures are harder to get right. Do you really think Jennie and Riley would take to being positioned and posed, and all that goes into a photo like the ones we're looking for?"

"Why would they have to pose? Can't you just snap as we're working? You're a pro, Hope. You'll come up with something that'll work."

Her lips dropped open as he unwittingly brushed aside all the hard work that went into her job, treating it as if it were nothing. "Something that will work? You're right about one thing, Blake. I *am* a pro. And if I'm going to put my name on something it's not going to be merely adequate. It has to be the best."

He stepped closer and she felt the proximity of his body practically vibrating against her. She had to tip her chin up to meet his gaze, and for one delicious moment his eyes dropped to her lips before moving back up to her eyes again.

"I'm not interested in perfection." His voice was an intense rumble in the quiet of the riding ring.

"And I never settle for anything less," she retorted.

"I bet you don't," he replied.

His voice was so *knowing* that she wanted to smack the snide smile off his perfectly shaped lips.

"How about compassion, Hope? Do you have any of that?"

If he'd reached out and slapped her it wouldn't have stung more. "Ouch," she said quietly. "You do know how to aim, don't you?"

He glowered at her. "Me with my scar. Jennie and Riley with their issues. Cate with her deformity. All of us—we come as a package deal. That's what Bighorn Therapeutic Riding is about. That's what you're hired to take pictures of. Not an empty barn."

Could he insult her any further? Goodness, she hadn't meant him—or the children. She'd meant perfection in *herself.*

She ignored the tiny voice that said he might be a little bit right and let her anger build up a head of steam. "Hired? I wasn't *hired.* I'm doing this for free, remember? You couldn't possibly afford what I charge an hour."

The indignant light in his eye dimmed and she felt like an utter heel for bringing money into it. He was doing a good thing here, and she knew his operating budget was probably a precise work of art from year to year. It had been a low blow. Maybe even lower than his dig about compassion.

It was only remembering his low opinion of her that kept her from apologizing—again.

"You're right, of course," he replied, his voice dangerously low.

"Take it or leave it."

Her words hung in the air for several seconds.

Blake stepped back, his eyes icy and his expression hard and closed-off. "Take your perfect pictures," he stated, then he smirked. "Oh, wait. You're *still* searching for the perfect shot. Good luck with that."

He spun on his boot heel and strode out of the ring leaving her standing there alone.

She looked down at her toes, trying to put her jumbled emotions in order, surprisingly stung by his harsh words. There was anger at being told how to do her job. Guilt for lashing out. And, most surprising of all, attraction. With their bodies close together and his gaze flashing at her there'd been a shiver of excitement that had zinged up her spine.

But all that aside the kicker was that he was right. She'd never accomplished perfection, no matter how hard she tried. She did settle for less—all the time. And, truth be told, seeking perfection was becoming rather exhausting.

Worse than that was that she knew how he'd taken her words. No one was perfect here, and that was the whole point. Everyone was scarred, flawed in some way. There was no cure. No permanent fix. There was just acceptance—and she'd essentially thrown that back in his face just now. He'd actually looked hurt underneath the angry set of his features. Because she hadn't just put down this place, she'd put *him* down too—even if it had been misconstrued. And she felt utterly rotten about it.

She had to fix it. Soon she'd be heading to Beckett's Run and Christmas with Gram. Somehow between now and then she'd find a way to give both herself and Blake what they wanted.

And then she'd get back to her previously scheduled life.

CHAPTER FIVE

T WASN'T often that Blake was in danger of losing his cool, but little Miss Perfect Pants had just about driven him there. He was used to people's misconceptions and, frankly, misunderstandings when it came to his work. He considered it part of his job to work to dispel them.

What he wasn't used to was this feeling of impotence that seemed to envelop him whenever Hope looked at his face. He hated that she could make him feel like a self-conscious boy all over again. The boy who'd been pitied at first, because of his tragedy, and then scorned for his appearance. Scorned and laughed at by his schoolmates, with adults frowning and shaking their heads in what he now recognized as condolence and sympathy. As if he'd died right along with his brother somehow. In some ways he'd preferred the teasing to people always feeling so damned sorry for him. At those times he had always felt like he was somehow too pitiful to be *worth* teasing.

And then there had been the girls who'd cringed when they looked at his face. He hadn't even gone to his own prom. He hadn't had a girlfriend and he hadn't wanted a pity date for the rite of passage either.

He'd grown older and wiser and had developed the confidence to know what he wanted to do with his life. Not everyone turned away in disgust. He'd even started dating along the way—and one relationship in particula he'd thought had potential. Until a few months in whe the offhand comments about his scar got more regula And then she'd suggested plastic surgery.

He'd never forgotten that moment. He'd thought tha girl was different. But she'd come right out and said it *You can't possibly want to go through life with that atroc ity on your face.*

Any dating he'd done since then had been short-lived. man couldn't live like a monk, but he never quite truste that anyone would see past his face to the man beneath And he could never accept anything less.

Hope McKinnon made him feel all those uncomfort able, powerless feelings again and he hated it. And h hated himself for letting her get to him and making hin say things he already regretted.

So he'd walked away before he could do any more dam age and left her in the ring to take her precious pictures

Now, an hour later, he pushed all his thoughts asid to focus on Cate Zerega. Cate was one of those childre who reached in and stole your heart without you seeing i coming. Dark curls touched her shoulders and enormou brown eyes dominated her face, but her body appeare twisted and her muscle control and coordination were im paired. Cerebral palsy had made it impossible for her t walk without forearm crutches, but it hadn't taken awa her bright smile, even though now and again her speec would slur when she was excited, Blake had accepted lon; ago that Cate was someone special.

When Cate had her appointments one of Blake's vol unteers attended, too. Shirley was a physiotherapist fron Canmore who had been donating her time for nearly tw years. Together with Cate's mom, Robbi, they formed strong team.

Today he'd saddled Queenie, one of the ponies he kept for the smaller children. Queenie was eighteen, and had never been overly ambitious. She was a dull gray, and not the prettiest equine specimen on the ranch, but she was gentle as a lamb and ten times as patient.

Cate's eyes lit up as Blake led Queenie to the ring.

"Hi, Mister Blake." Cate's eyes were round as dollars and Blake's earlier irritation slipped away.

"Hey, cupcake. You ready to ride?"

She nodded. "I've been waiting all week."

Her words were clear, with only the slightest hitch.

She gave her crutches to her mother and Blake lifted her in his arms. He took in a breath and was enveloped in a sweet cloud of little girl smell…strawberry shampoo, fabric softener and what he guessed was a fruity sort of snack eaten during their drive out from Calgary.

As gently as possible he settled her in the saddle. There you go, munchkin. Queenie's all ready for you." He reached up and made sure the black helmet was secure on her head, then gave it two knocks with his knuckles.

"Who's there?" she asked.

"Ya," he said solemnly.

"Ya-who?" she asked, equally sober.

"Yahoo? Are you a cowboy, too?"

She giggled and he saw Robbi roll her eyes as she grinned. "Do you two never get tired of that joke?" she asked.

"Nope," Cate answered for them both.

Blake looked at Shirley and Robbi. "She's ready to go. Shall I lead first?"

They started the session in the ring, Blake leading Queenie around the perimeter while Shirley and Robbie walked along on either side. They stopped occasionally to adjust, and invariably Cate gave Queenie a pat on her mane before they started again. Blake smiled. Cate had improved since starting here months earlier, due to the simple act of riding. It got her blood pumping, helped with her core strength, posture and muscle tone.

"I think she's ready," Shirley said quietly, and Blake halted the team.

"Your turn," he said to Cate. "My arm's tired. Do you think you could take the reins now?"

She nodded. "I can."

"That's good news. Now, your mom will be right beside you. Just take her in a nice slow walk around the ring, okay?"

He put the reins in her hand, ensuring they were even and secure before stepping back. "I'm going to watch from over here."

He backed off and watched as Cate seemed to sit up even straighter from the simple act of being in charge. He smiled to himself. It was amazing what a little confidence and pride could do. She loved being in control of Queenie, even if it was just plodding around the ring endlessly at a walk.

"I'm doing it, Mister Blake!" she called out.

"You sure are!" he shouted back. "Good job, sweetie!"

Something caught the corner of his eye. He looked over and saw Hope, her camera raised, clicking away.

She lowered the camera and caught his eye. Something passed between them; something wordless and honest and accepting. It was an apology from Hope, a willingness to bend demonstrated by her returning to the ring to take some shots of Cate.

Blake dipped his head in a subtle nod—a tacit thank you and his own apology—and the tension and bitterness that had snapped between them earlier melted away.

Instead something else hummed in the air between

them—something warm and exciting. He now understood why he'd felt as he had earlier—powerless. He wasn't in high school anymore but it was the same jumped-up feeling he'd gotten when he'd liked a girl...when he'd been attracted to someone...and when he'd considered that someone out of his league. Back then the girls had always looked away when he'd met their eyes.

The difference now was that despite her angry words Hope wasn't looking away. She was looking directly at him. No flinching. And as the seconds spun out he started thinking about her long blond hair, and the blue of her eyes that was clear as a glacier stream, and her long thoroughbred legs. He loved that she was so tall. So... He swallowed. *Accessible.* At six foot five, he usually towered over women—and a number of men, too.

"Good girl, Queenie!"

He snapped out of the moment at Cate's cheerful words as horse, rider and entourage passed by. He heard the clicking of Hope's camera as the group passed close to where she was standing.

Blake shoved his hands in his pockets. He was a smart man. He knew well enough what was going on. Curiosity. Awareness. Back and forth arguing that set off sparks in both of them.

And strategic retreat—him to the barn and her behind the lens of her camera.

But it was there all the same. The big question was, would he be smart and do nothing?

Or stupid and see what would happen?

He kept his gaze on horse and rider. He wasn't—and never had been—a stupid man.

Hope blinked furiously against the stinging in her eyes and focused on what she saw within the frame of her camera. She took picture after picture of the little girl sitting atop the aging pony. That was what Blake had asked of her and that was what she was going to do.

Even if it hurt. Even if parts of her heart that she'd thought closed off years before were coming slowly, painfully to life at the sight of the gruff rancher smiling at a poppet of a girl on a horse.

She hadn't known he could be this way.

But she'd keep the camera focused on the little girl and pony, even though she was tempted to turn around and take pictures of Blake. The way he rested his weight on one hip. The soulful expression in his eyes as he gave her that tiny no-fuss nod. The way his eyes lit up and his smile broke over his face like a prairie dawn when he spoke to the child on the pony.

She was far too aware of Blake, so she resolutely kept her eye on the team of people in the center of the ring and not on Blake on the sidelines.

When the session ended Blake moved forward and took the reins. He led the horse and rider to the edge of the ring and the concrete floor. Hope stayed to the side, still snapping, as one woman retrieved the forearm crutches and Blake reached up and lifted the girl from the saddle. He put her down carefully and helped her with the crutches.

Hope swallowed tightly. The girl wore small brown boots, and with the black riding helmet looked like the perfect tiny equestrian. The way she was looking up at Blake was pure hero-worship. And why not? He was a big, strong man who treated her with gentleness and kindness. He was good with kids. No, more than good. He was a natural, and it made her long for something she had stopped hoping for years ago. For someone—for *him*—to turn that gentleness on her. To make her feel as special, as treasured, as the little girl on the pony.

The center of someone's world.

"There you go. Time to put Queenie away."

"Mom says there's no more lessons until after Christmas."

Blake tipped back his hat and squatted down in front of her. "That's right. Everyone gets a bit of a vacation over the holidays."

"But I don't want a vacation," Cate said, her lower lip pouting just a bit.

Hope hid a smile, but didn't turn away from the scene.

Blake smiled at Cate. "Well, you're in luck. Because next week instead of riding we're doing something else."

"We are?"

He nodded. "Yep. Next week we're having a Christmas party."

"With cookies?"

"Of course."

"And hot chocolate?"

"Naturally."

Cate used her crutches to step closer, and Hope couldn't hold back the smile now, even as the sight of her sent a pang through Hope's heart. The girl was playing Blake like a violin. Whatever she asked for Blake would probably agree just because she'd asked it.

"And Queenie?"

His smile fell. "Nope, not Queenie." He waited a beat and then added, "But better. We're going on a sleigh ride."

"A sleigh ride?" The excitement was back. "With bells on the horses?"

He slapped a hand to his forehead. "I plumb forgot about bells."

"You can't have a sleigh ride without bells."

Hope heard how excitement put a slight lag on the girl's

speech. How could anyone remain immune to such an enchanting creature?

Hope stepped forward, her heart pounding with uncertainty. "If there are bells to be had, Blake'll find them." She smiled tentatively.

The dark eyes were turned up at her now. "He will?"

It was such an honest, heartfelt question that Hope didn't stand a chance either. Hard as she might try to keep her distance while she was here, there was something about this little girl that reminded her of herself at that age. She blinked as she realized it was her name— Hope. Cate had it in spades. And Hope missed having that trusting innocence.

"Has Blake ever let you down before?"

Cate shook her head.

"Well, there you go, then."

The girl turned back to Blake with more questions and Hope straightened. She turned to the pair of women looking on and smiling.

"Hi," she said, holding out her hand. "I'm Hope McKinnon. I'm doing some photography for promotional materials. I wondered if it would be okay to use today's shots? I'll have an official release drawn up, but for now your okay would be great."

"I'm Shirley, and of course you can. I'm a physiotherapist from Canmore, and I volunteer to work with a lot of Blake's more physically challenged clients."

"Then *you* must be the mom of this angel," Hope said, shaking the other woman's hand. "She's got Blake wrapped around her little finger, hasn't she?"

"Oh, and the other way around, too. I'm Robbi, and I'm happy to let you use any photos you like of today, Ms. McKinnon. Anything to help the facility. This place means a lot to Cate and our family. It's just wonderful."

They chatted a few minutes more. Out of the corner of her eye Hope saw Blake remove Queenie's tack while Cate, using her crutches, followed him like a faithful pup, keeping a safe distance as instructed, chattering the entire time. Hero-worship indeed. What was amazing was that Blake didn't seem the least bit fizzed by her incessant talk. He looked like he enjoyed it.

At the end he grabbed an apple, took out a jackknife and cut it into quarters, and then knelt beside Cate on the concrete floor. "You want to give Queenie a treat now?"

Cate let go of one of her crutches and balanced on the other, then held out the apple on the palm of her hand. Queenie lapped it up and crunched lazily while Cate laughed.

Robbi sighed. "Every time I see them together I wonder why that man isn't married with a bunch of his own kids."

Something seemed to expand in Hope's chest. She'd never even thought to ask if Blake had a girlfriend or if he was interested in anyone. Did Robbi have designs on him? She wondered how many of the moms talked about Blake like he was the next best thing to sliced bread. The idea made her feel unusually plain and un-special—especially as she was already aware that she stood a whole head taller than this very attractive mom.

Robbi laughed. "If I weren't already happily married…"

Well. That answered *that* question. Robbi looked at Shirley.

"You coming to the sleigh ride?"

Shirley shook her head. "Afraid not. We're heading to Cranbrook for Christmas the day before."

"Have a good holiday, then." Robbi called to her daughter, "Are you ready, honey?"

"Awwww," Cate complained, "do we have to?"

Robbi looked at Hope. "And this is why we love it here.

School is a bit of a challenge this year, but when she's here she seems so incredibly typical. Does that make sense?"

Hope smiled. "It does. Thanks for your permission."

"You bet. See you at the sleigh ride?"

Hope had been thinking she would give it a miss, but now she was curious. And she was thinking. She didn't normally do candid shots, but what if she did some at the party? If none of them turned out well, she wouldn't have to use them. But there'd never be a better chance to get a variety of clients all together. Staging shots was difficult, but one group shot might be doable. If nothing else she could give it to Blake as a present. She got the feeling he'd like something like that.

"Yes, I'll be there," she replied.

"Be where?" Blake's voice said behind her shoulder.

She turned and pinned on a bright smile. "At the sleigh ride, of course. I wouldn't miss it."

His eyebrow was raised. She suspected it was half in surprise and half unspoken challenge. "You're sure? It's going to be hectic."

It was her turn to raise an eyebrow. "You're forgetting I deal with temperamental models all day. If I can handle the divas, I think I can handle this."

He grinned. "Suit yourself. And in that case…"

"What?"

"Oh, nothing. Yet. I'm still working on some ideas."

He moved off to say goodbye to the group.

What ideas? And why did she have a very bad feeling they were going to involve something she didn't want to do?

For the rest of the week Hope and Blake managed to form a truce. Quite often Anna ran interference between them in the house during the day, contributing to the status quo, and Hope spent a lot of time in and around the barn taking pictures.

As she watched during Saturday's session it continually amazed her how hands-on Blake was with the kids, and how he genuinely enjoyed working with them—even when things didn't go particularly well. She'd started thinking along the same lines as Cate's mom—why on earth hadn't he married and started his own family? Clearly he liked kids. He was stable, secure…and despite the scar on his face not bad to look at either. For the right woman he'd be quite the catch—so what was the holdup?

Of course *she* wasn't that woman. Marriage, kids, the whole settling down thing? The very idea scared her to death. She'd already attempted to raise one family and hadn't done such a great job of it. It wasn't something she wanted to screw up twice.

She focused on the job. Soon she'd really have to sit down and start organizing the photos—picking and choosing the best ones and doing some editing. But for now, in the evenings, she found herself more often than not alone in the house while Blake spent his time in the barn. He was painting the sleigh and getting things ready for the party, he explained. There was always a glint in his eye when he mentioned it, and she was afraid to ask what had put it there. Truth be told, she was enjoying her evenings of solitude. A cup of tea and a book or a DVD while curled up next to a blazing fire was not a bad way to spend an evening. Whenever she felt like she was being indulgent she thought of Gram. Gram would be happy to know she was taking some downtime, if that was her worry.

Sometimes, before she went to bed, Blake would come and sit for an hour and watch a program with her. During those times they'd let the television do the talking. It was amazing to Hope how they were both comfortable to do so.

* * *

Anna had taken the day off to finish up her Christmas shopping.

Hope wandered downstairs at half-past nine, dressed in pyjama pants and a sweatshirt. The sun was bright and the light through the windows was diamond-sharp as it glinted off the snow. She squinted her way to the coffee-pot, and was pouring her first fragrant cup when Blake came through from the laundry room.

"Hey, sleepyhead," he said, reaching for a mug.

"You're too cheerful for this early in the morning," she remarked, affecting a scowl.

He chuckled. "Chores done, *and* I threw a load of laundry in."

"Disgusting," she commented, but his good mood was contagious. She took a sip of coffee and closed her eyes. The man did know how to brew a decent cup of joe.

"I haven't eaten yet, and my morning appointment has cancelled today. Doctor's appointment. You hungry?"

"I guess."

"Great." He reached beneath the cupboard and plunked an appliance on the countertop.

"What on earth is that?"

"A griddle. I'm making French toast. I told you it's my specialty."

Her mouth began to water. "Real French toast? Like dipped in egg batter and drowned in maple syrup?"

"Of course. And bacon to go with it."

Sweet mother—bacon, too? She'd be as big as a house after ten days of eating this way—first Anna's fine cooking and now Blake's. "I love bacon."

"Then you're in charge of that." He grabbed a pound from the fridge and got her a frying pan. "Cook it all. I'll use what's left for BLTs later."

They worked around the kitchen easily, Hope turning

the bacon and putting the crisp pieces to drain on paper towel while Blake mixed up milk and eggs. Out of the corner of her eye she saw him add vanilla and cinnamon. The first slice of French bread soon sizzled on the griddle, and as it cooked Blake got real maple syrup out of the fridge, along with butter and orange juice. When the slices were done he put them in the oven to stay warm and repeated the process.

When all the bread was gone and the bacon was cooked, they sat down at the kitchen table to eat. The earth was frozen and white outside the windows, but inside Hope was warm and relaxed. There really was something about this place. The dominance of natural wood in the design and the rustic decor was growing on her, and her new favorite thing was the stone hearth and the flue for the fireplace.

It was about as far removed from her modern apartment in Sydney as you could get, but there was something here that her apartment would never have. She looked around and realized it was permanence—rock and logs and land. This place was built to last. The people here *stayed* here. The reality of that was foreign to Hope, but the dream wasn't. It was what she'd searched for her whole childhood and never found.

She'd given up believing in it, but Blake lived it every day. She wondered if he appreciated it.

And yet…his parents weren't here. They'd gone off to warmer climes and sunnier days. There was no wife, no babies bouncing on his knee. Maybe Hope was only seeing what she wanted to see. She certainly had a habit of doing that. How many times over the years had she painted castles in the air only to have them tumble back to earth again?

How many times had she put her trust in people only to have them let her down?

He turned on the radio and a local station played country music interspersed with Christmas carols. Hope poured syrup on her toast and took the first delicious bite. When was the last time she'd had French toast? Probably the last time she'd had breakfast at the pancake house in Beckett's Run. She'd always put maple syrup on the first piece, and then load the second with icing sugar and whipped cream and fruit for "dessert."

Good memories. She took a hasty sip of juice to hide an unexpected burst of emotion. So many of her memories were tied up in anger and disappointment that it was a revelation to have such a simple, positive one pop up out of the blue.

"What are you smiling at?" Blake asked, helping himself to bacon off the plate.

She cut another piece of toast, savouring the rich vanilla and cinnamon flavor. "I was just remembering going to the pancake house in the town where Gram lives. She'd take us there when we were kids and we'd eat until we were nearly sick. This brought back memories, that's all."

"You spent a lot of time with your grandmother?"

She nodded as she finished chewing and swallowed. "We moved around a lot as kids, but we spent holidays and summers at Gram's. That's the real home I remember."

"What about your mom and dad?"

She shrugged, determined not to let things get dark and depressing. It was what it was, and nothing would change it now. "They were on again, off again a lot. My mom's a free spirit type, and my dad's more…*traditional,*" she finished. "For lack of a better word. He always wanted her to settle down and face reality. She wanted him to lighten up. There was a lot of friction. They went their own ways a lot."

"But…?"

Explaining her family dynamic had always been a challenge. "But they usually tried again. It was pretty confusing. Hard on my younger sisters, mostly, I think. Faith was shy and didn't say much, and Grace tended to act out for attention."

"And you?"

She put down her fork and picked up her coffee, half hiding behind the cup and curls of steam. "Oh, me," she said easily. Perhaps too easily to be believable. "I tried to help where I could."

Which was the grandest understatement of the century. She'd tried to provide the stability that the three girls had been missing. And, as much as she'd understood her mom's need to spread her wings, she'd wished in the deepest corners of her heart that her dad would come and sweep them all home and tell Lydia that this was enough nonsense.

She'd wanted them to be a regular family. Desperately.

"You've gone quiet," he observed softly.

She cleared her throat and busied herself cutting into her breakfast. "Never mind," she said briskly. "Look, Blake. I've seen the kids that you work with all week. I could boo-hoo about my past all I want, but the truth is, I've never had to deal with what those kids and parents are dealing with. I just need to get over myself, and that's that."

His wide hand closed over hers and the fork stilled. "That is easier said than done, and I know it."

She stared at his fingers, at the way they completely dwarfed her hand, how strong they felt wrapped around her skin, and before she could think about what a bad idea it was she turned her wrist so that her hand rolled and their fingers clasped together.

Not just a gesture of comfort now, but a real, honest-to-goodness physical link between them, and Hope felt it clear to her toes.

His thumb rubbed against her wrist, warm and reassuring, and she made no effort to pull away. Just another few moments. It felt so good to feel like a part of something, even if it was as simple as holding hands at a breakfast table. She'd been alone a long time. By choice, but alone just the same.

"*You* got over yourself," she reminded him. "You didn't let your accident stop you."

His fingers tightened on hers. "Didn't I? There were a lot of years between the injury and starting this place. I felt plenty sorry for myself. Plenty guilty."

"Guilty?" Hope looked up into his face. "What on earth did you have to feel guilty about?"

His eyes were the saddest she'd seen them as he said, "My brother was in the car, too. He didn't make it."

CHAPTER SIX

"Didn't make it?"

Hope felt like she needed to pull her hand away, but she couldn't. It would be a deliberate withdrawal and a step back—not at all what she should do at this moment.

Blake had had a brother? She swallowed. As much as she'd argued with her sisters, having them had always been a blessing. Because of them she'd never felt alone. Despite the strain of the responsibility she'd felt, and it hadn't been easy, they'd been there, given her a purpose. Even if they'd acted out in their own ways, the reason for it had tied them together.

She couldn't imagine what it would have been like to lose one of them.

"I'm so sorry," she whispered. "That must have been terrible for you."

"Brad was my twin," he said roughly. "We did everything together. The bond between twins is…"

"I've heard it's different. That the connection is deeper."

"I knew what he was thinking, sometimes what he was feeling. We played hockey together and sometimes we were so in tune with each other it was like music." He pulled his hand away then, and gave a sad smile. "I think of him when I watch the Sedin brothers play now. We could have been like that."

Hope didn't know who the Sedin brothers were but she didn't need to know to understand that Blake still felt the loss keenly.

"I can't imagine not having my sisters," Hope replied. "You're close?"

She looked down at her plate, annoyed with herself for bringing the conversation back to herself when she really wanted to learn more about him.

"Not particularly. But…I know they're there."

She suddenly felt guilty about not keeping in touch more. Not making more of an effort now that they were all grown up and leading their own lives. Faith and Grace weren't her responsibility any longer, but instead of trying to redefine their relationship, they'd drifted apart. Anytime either of them had asked her for anything she'd turned her back. Maybe it was time that changed.

"I spent a lot of time wishing for Brad back," Blake said. "It felt like a piece of me was missing. And I really struggled with why he was taken and I was left behind. At the same time I was a teenager, going through all the things that teens go through. We'd talked about going to the NHL together. All the dreams and plans were ours, and without him I had nothing."

"So what did you do?" She looked up at him, feeling strangely bereft at the grief still shadowing his voice. Had Blake hit rock bottom like she had?

"Got by day to day. Lived in a shell. Shut people out."

Hope's throat swelled as she remembered the day she'd finally given up on holding her family together. She'd broken down, and Gram had been there to pick up the pieces, but things had been different from that point on. Ever since she'd kept people at arm's length. She wasn't blind. She knew that if she didn't let anyone too close she didn't have to worry about disappointments or goodbyes.

Blake had come out of his shell and built this place. She hadn't, and she hid behind a camera.

"How did you come out of it?"

Blake had, and he'd done something extraordinary.

"My dad." Blake seemed to relax, and resumed cutting into what was left of his pile of French toast. "He and Mom took the accident hard. It was awful around here. But he showed up in the barn one day and handed me a pair of skates. I hadn't played hockey in three years—the accident ended my season and I never went back. He told me he'd lost one son and he'd be damned if he'd lose another and told me to put on the skates."

"And you did?"

He grinned. The way his mouth pulled made him look rakish. "You haven't met my dad. You don't argue with him. We went to the pond over at Anna and John's, laced up our skates and took shots at a net for three hours."

He mopped up some syrup with a chunk of bread.

"After that I spent some time deciding what I wanted to do. I read an article about the therapeutic benefits of riding and it clicked. The one thing I'd done through it all was work with the horses. They were my saving grace. The more I looked into it, the more I knew. And when Dad retired I made it a reality."

Hope pushed away her nearly empty plate. "You're very good at what you do, Blake. And very good with kids. I'm kind of surprised you don't have any of your own."

His gaze touched hers. "Been wondering about me, have you?"

"Don't flatter yourself," she replied, feeling heat rise in her cheeks. "I'm not the only one to speculate. Half the women that walk through your stable doors wonder the same thing."

His eyes looked confused for a moment, but then they

cleared and he brushed off her observation. "Women don't tend to be interested in a man like me."

"What's that supposed to mean?"

His blue gaze pinned her again. "You know. They take one look at my face and…" He put his knife and fork on top of his plate. "It's a lot to get past."

Was he serious? Hope didn't know what to say. Sure, she'd reacted to his scar, but she hardly noticed it now. It was hidden by his other fine qualities. His kindness, the way he smiled at the children, the light in his eyes and the strong, sure way he carried himself. Once she'd seen him in his element she'd glimpsed the real Blake. He was the kind of man who could be quite dangerous to a woman like her.

She could reassure him, but that would reveal way too much, so she came up with the only paltry platitude possible. "Someday the right woman will come along and sweep you off your feet." She smiled. "You'll see."

She pushed back her chair and picked up her plate. But Blake caught her wrist as she went to move past him.

His fingers were strong and sure as they circled her wrist. "This place is the most important thing to me right now. And I haven't said it yet, but thank you for what you're doing. You were right. I couldn't afford you by the hour."

She stared into his honest face. "I'm sorry I ever said that. You touched a nerve that day with the perfect thing."

He let go of her wrist. "I know I did."

"Not the way you think," she answered. "It's not *you* I expect to be perfect, Blake, or the children, or anyone else except me. It's *me* who keeps falling short of the mark."

That little bombshell dropped, she escaped to the sink to rinse off her plate.

She heard the scrape of his chair as he pushed back

from the table, knew he was behind her. She kept her back to him, the water running uselessly in the sink now that her plate was rinsed.

"There are things in life that happen and that we can't see coming. That's just reality," he said, his voice quiet but full of conviction. "Expecting yourself to be perfect is setting yourself up to fail."

"How can you say that?" she asked, turning back around and facing him. "How can you, when you are so good at what you do? Do you even have any flaws, Blake? And I don't mean physical ones."

"Plenty," he whispered. "I'm far from perfect, Hope. I just try to stay on the positive side. To find joy in things."

"But sometimes the heartache doesn't allow you to trust in the joy," she replied. "Because you know it could be ripped away at any moment."

There was a long silence. Finally he lifted his hand and placed his palm along her cheek. "I look at you and I know that there are many ways to grieve without having experienced death. What are you grieving for, Hope?"

"When my friend Julie died…" She scrambled to put together the words, but he shook his head. His hand was warm, comforting on her skin and she bit down on her lip so it wouldn't tremble.

"No, it's more than that. There's something else. Something you lost and never got back."

She blinked and sidestepped away from his hand, away from his eyes. "Don't," she warned. "I told you when I first got here not to go all shrink on me, remember?"

"I just want to help."

"Then leave me alone. Let me be, Blake, please. It's been a good week. I took some pictures and got fresh air and I've relaxed. Just let that be enough, okay? In a few days we have the sleigh ride, and then I fly out to Boston."

"For a family Christmas?"

"Yes. Let's just chill for the next few days, okay? No more digging into our personal lives. I won't if you won't."

She wanted to know more about him, but fair was fair. She couldn't expect him to open up while she remained a closed door, could she?

There was a long pause, and then Blake's shoulders dropped. "Okay."

"Okay. Now, since you cooked I'll tidy up. And this afternoon I'm going to start going through the pictures I have. Layout's not my specialty, but I'll put together a portfolio of shots you can take to a good designer."

"I've got a few jobs to do, as well. I'll be back by midafternoon. Maybe you can show me then."

"That'd be good."

He looked like he wanted to say something more, but then he shook his head. "All right. See you later."

"Later."

When she saw him again she was sitting at the table listening to the hum of the dishwasher, her laptop open before her. Her gaze caught a glimpse of a thick red hat above his black ski jacket. He wore heavy pants, too, and she gathered that whatever he was going to do it was going to be out in the bitter December weather. He'd be cold when he got back in. Maybe she'd make some cocoa to warm him up.

She shivered and turned back to her photos. Scratch the cocoa. After this morning she'd realized she was spending far too much time concerned about Blake's welfare. She could still feel the gentle touch of his hand along the side of her face. *Aw, hell.* She was starting to care for him more than she was comfortable with. When he'd talked about his brother her heart had cracked just a bit, and she'd had the crazy urge to take him in her arms and comfort him.

Which made her just about as starstruck as the moms who gazed at him like he was perfection in a cowboy hat.

He'd seen it on their snowmobile ride, and now Blake trudged the last hundred feet into the barnyard, towing the toboggan behind him. The perfect Christmas tree—eight feet of spruce, perfectly tapered, just the right size for the vaulted ceiling in the family room—was sprawled over it. A good shaking to get the snow off, a couple of taps with the hatchet on the trunk and it would be ready for the tree stand.

He expected Hope would balk at the idea of putting up a tree, but he wanted it up for the Christmas party, and his parents would be arriving Christmas Eve. He gave the rope a hard tug and pulled the toboggan over a small snowbank. If she didn't want to help decorate, that was fine. He'd done it by himself lots of times. Usually with a hockey game on in the background.

He'd seen the look of longing in Hope's eyes this morning, though. Felt the squeeze of her fingers in his. She wasn't as immune as she wanted him to believe. And everyone deserved to have a good dose of Christmas spirit. It didn't have to go any further than that. Shouldn't. No matter how attractive he'd found her.

No matter how much she'd surprised him by saying what she had this morning.

Her reaction to his face had been the worst, but now she was acting as though it didn't matter anymore.

Well, *fool me once,* as the saying went. They were just words, after all.

But it didn't change the fact that he sensed she was sad and wanted to cheer her up. He knew what it was like to be in that abyss. So he'd dig out the decorations and make the best of it.

He stood the tree on the porch and went inside, clomping his boots to get the snow off before disappearing into the basement to the storage area for the stand. When he came back up, Hope was looking down the staircase curiously.

"What are you up to?"

He held up the stand. "Christmas tree. Wanna help?"

Just as he'd expected, she took a step back. "You were out getting a tree?"

"Of course. After the sleigh ride we'll have cookies and hot chocolate in here. The kids will expect a tree."

He didn't mention the second part of the plan—the part where he'd be dressing up like Santa Claus and needing an elf. He wanted to hit her with it at the right moment, and give her as little chance as possible to try and get out of it.

"Oh."

She stepped aside, but he handed her the stand and bent to unlace his boots. He looked up as he shrugged out of his jacket and hung it on a peg.

She looked awkward and uncertain, and he smiled on the inside. "Come on," he prodded, nudging her through the door and toward the family room. "Help me move some furniture to make room."

Together they rearranged the furniture that sat next to the fireplace by moving the sofa down a bit and shifting a heavy side table to the other corner, pushing it against a matching table so that it made one wide rectangular surface. Blake eyeballed the vacant space and put down the tree stand in the precise spot he wanted it.

"You loosen the screws and I'll bring in the tree," he suggested, and without waiting for her response went out on the porch in his stockinged feet and picked up the spruce.

Together they fit the tree into the stand, and he held it level while Hope knelt on the floor and tightened the wing nuts. When it was secure she stood up, and he stepped back, admiring. It was the perfect fit. The perfect amount of fullness except for one spot that was a little sparse. He turned that side toward the wall—problem solved.

"Oh, my gosh, that smells so good!" Hope exclaimed, brushing off her hands.

"Wait until we get lights on it," he said, finally feeling some Christmas spirit. There was nothing like the scent of a real tree to put you in the holiday mood.

"I haven't had a real tree since…"

"Since?" She'd hesitated, leaving the sentence incomplete. Good memories or bad ones? he wondered.

"Since our family Christmases with my grandmother."

He looked over at her and caught her smiling wistfully.

"We always had a real tree, too. And Gram did her holiday baking and the kitchen always smelled good."

"You don't have a real tree now?"

She shook her head. "I live in an apartment and I travel a lot. A small artificial one is enough."

"Not this year, eh?" he asked, thinking that the idea of spending the holidays alone in an apartment with a plastic tree sounded very lonely indeed. "I'll go bring up the boxes of decorations." He nodded at the television. "There's a Christmas Classics channel in the music section. Why don't you turn it on?"

"Really?"

She sounded skeptical, and that just wouldn't do.

"You can't decorate without Christmas carols," he decreed.

By the time he found the boxes and got them upstairs Christmas songs were playing and Hope had disappeared.

"Hope?"

"In the kitchen."

Her voice came from around the corner, and he put the first box in the living room before going to find her.

She was standing in front of the stove, stirring something in a pot that smelled fantastically spicy.

"Mulled cider," she announced. "I found the seasonings when I was looking in the cupboard the other day. This is as good a time as any, right?"

"It's perfect. I'll start on the lights while you finish up. The lights take the longest."

He was halfway through putting multi-colored twinkle lights on the tree when she came into the room carrying two mugs, steam curling off the top. He took a break and stood up, stretching out his back as she held out the mug.

"It looks good," she offered.

"I like lots of lights," he replied, thinking back to when he and Brad had been boys and their job had been to stand back and squint. The lights had all blurred together, and any blank spots in their vision had meant there were holes that needed to be filled. One year the tree had been so big that their dad had used over fifteen hundred lights on it. "It's kind of a family tradition."

He took a sip of his cider and raised his eyebrows. "Mmmm," he remarked, angling a sideways glance at Hope.

Her lips were twitching just a little.

"I found some spiced rum in the cupboard, too. Thought it might warm you up after your cold hike."

He swallowed the warm cider, felt the kick of the rum in his belly. It wasn't just the rum. It was her, wasn't it? She could have a fun side if she let it out to play more. She put a wall around herself most of the time, but behind that wall he had a suspicion there was hidden a warm, giving woman. A woman he could like. A lot.

Right now she looked barely past twenty, with her straight hair in a perky ponytail and hardly any makeup. He could think of more pleasant ways than mulled cider to warm up, and all of them included her, in his arms.

Which would be a very, very bad idea. They were hardly even friends. It was a big leap from their new-found civility to being lovers. And there was no point in starting something he didn't intend to finish.

"It's good," was all he said, and he took another drink for fortification. It didn't help that she looked so cute in her snug jeans, when her long fingers curled around the mug as she blew on the hot surface of the cider with full pink lips.

He got to work putting on the rest of the lights while she dug through the boxes for ornaments and the tacky red and green tinsel garland he put on the tree each year. By the time he'd finished she'd pulled out a box and was sitting on the sofa, surrounded by nearly a dozen porcelain shops and buildings—his mother's Christmas village.

"This is adorable," she said, lifting up an ornament that depicted a red square building with a steeply pitched roof and the word *Schoolhouse* on a sign above the door.

"My mom's. Every year we got her a different building until she could build a whole town. Look." He reached inside a large plastic ice cream container and took out a tiny LED light. "Put this inside and it lights up."

"Pretty. Where do you normally put it?"

"On the long table in the hall."

Hope held the porcelain carefully in her hands and looked up at him, dismay turning her lips downward. "But you can't enjoy it there. You only see it as you pass through." She looked around and then her eyes lit up. "Look. What about the two tables we pushed together?"

"It's big enough."

"We need a white cloth. Just a minute."

She disappeared upstairs and returned with a snowy white towel. He watched as she draped it over the tables and put the schoolhouse down. She stood back and put a finger to her lips, then went back to the box again and again. She went into the kitchen and came back with something in her hand he couldn't discern, but she tucked it under the towel and before his eyes a hill of snow seemed to appear. Tiny figurines of children followed, punctuated by green bottlebrush-like trees and a snowman in a black top hat. Before he knew it she'd arranged the whole village—church, school, bookshop, houses—along the table, with snowy white hills forming a backdrop.

"How did you do that?"

She beamed. "Do you like it?"

"I do. What's more, I think my mom will, too. It's a shame you're not going to meet her."

Not meet her…not be here for Christmas Eve and then Christmas morning…it surprised him to realize he wanted her there. He liked having Anna around, but there was something right about Hope being in the house, wandering through the barns. She added something to the place—a sense of sophistication and class that he found he appreciated. And ever since that first day with Cate he'd been able to tell that even when she held back, there was something about the children that she responded to. She was fitting in rather well, considering the hoity-toity photographer who'd arrived only days ago.

Perhaps fitting in too well. Considering lately he couldn't stop thinking about her.

* * *

Hope saw the look in Blake's eyes and nerves bubbled in her tummy. She'd seen that look before: a softening of the features, a warming of the eyes, the slight parting of lips. There were times she tried to elicit this precise expression for the camera. Other times she'd seen it in the moments before she'd been kissed.

And Blake was looking at *her* that way, making her knees turn to jelly and her pulse pound.

Kissing him would not be the smartest move. All it would do was complicate things. This was supposed to be an easy ten days, then off to Gram's for Christmas and back to her life in Sydney, just as she'd created it. Granted, she'd been thinking about him a lot. Granted, she'd had to move past her own "rules" and face some old demons in order to give him what he wanted for the facility. That had put her out of her comfort zone.

Funny how out of her comfort zone it seemed kind of… well, cozy and right.

But in the end everything would go back to normal— which was Hope looking after Hope and not fretting about everyone else. Not getting involved.

She suspected that kissing Blake was definitely something a girl wouldn't walk away from without fretting on some level, so she nodded toward the boxes, breaking the spell of the moment while the music station shifted to a horrendous version of "O Holy Night."

"We should probably put on the rest of the decorations. Are they in this box?"

The warm intensity of his eyes cooled and he stepped back. "Oh, right." He opened the box and pulled out the bag that had ropes of red and green garland poking out of the top. "This is next."

It was tacky and cheap and slightly gaudy to Hope's artist's eye. Still, it was his tree, his house. And having grown up with Gram she did hold the slightest remnant of knowledge that traditions were not to be messed with—especially on the holidays. She took the first mass of tinsel in her hands and began looping it around the tree in a precise scallop pattern while Blake held the end.

"You're very exact."

She frowned and adjusted a swoop of garland. "I like things balanced. If they're imbalanced they have to be intentionally so, you know?"

"Not exactly. But you're having fun with it, so go for it."

He was teasing her now, and she didn't know whether to be pleased or annoyed.

Together they added ornaments to the tree—cutesy homemade types that were hand-painted or stitched: old-fashioned gingerbread men and knitted skates and bells, red and green boots with paperclips as blades, and gold-shot yarn bells with tiny brass jingle bells dangling from the centre, catching the light of the bulbs.

It was a long way from her red-and-white tree and the delicate glass balls that she had at home.

It was, she realized, a family tree. A tree with years of memories and love. And Blake was here alone. His brother was gone and he was stuck decorating the tree with a stranger.

Well, not exactly a stranger—not anymore. But definitely not family.

She wondered if the tree was up at Gram's. Wondered what Beckett's Run looked like, dressed for the holidays. Wondered if Gram had baked Hope's favorite holiday cookies—the chocolatey ones in powdered sugar.

Good heavens. She was homesick.

"Are you all right?" Blake's voice brought her back to earth and she realized she was standing holding an ornament, the string looped over her finger.

"Oh. Of course. Just thinking."

"About what?"

She drew in a breath that was shakier than she liked. "It's silly, really. I was just remembering Christmas in Beckett's Run. No matter what was going on in our lives, we always went home for Christmas."

"Good memories, then?"

She nodded. "Mostly."

She hung the ornament and saw Blake was holding a small oval one in his hands. His face changed, a mixture of love and pain twisting his features. When he'd hung it gently on the tree she could see it was a photo frame, and when she stepped she closer realized it was black with a big red "C" on it—the logo of the Calgary Flames. Inside the frame was a picture of two boys in oversize jerseys, hockey sticks on the ice, grinning widely for the camera.

Blake and his brother, Brad. Eleven, maybe twelve years old. Blake without the jagged scar down the side of his face, before puberty hit full force. His twin, Brad, looking so much like Blake it was uncanny, but with something different around the eyes and mouth.

She touched her finger to Blake's figure. "That's you, right?"

"Not everyone could tell us apart."

"It's the eyes and the shape of your mouth. And you're big as a barn door now, Blake…stands to reason maybe you were a little taller than Brad."

"I was the better checker," he said softly, "but Brad had faster hands."

"I'm sorry."

"You have nothing to be sorry about." He stared at the photo a while longer. "It is what it is. I miss him every day. But nothing will bring him back. I stopped making those sorts of wishes long ago. Now I just remember."

"And put this ornament on the tree?"

Blake's mouth twisted, and once more Hope noticed how the stiffness of his scar pulled his lips slightly. She wondered how horrible it must have been for him as a teen, dealing with that sort of disfiguration. Dealing with people's reactions. It wasn't much wonder he'd been curt with her when she'd arrived. The first thing she'd done was stare at him like he was some sort of freak.

But he wasn't. He was the strongest man she'd ever met.

"There's just one thing left to do," he said, clearing his throat. "Put the angel on the top."

He reached into the box and took out a rectangular carton. He opened the flap and carefully took out the most beautiful Christmas angel Hope had ever seen. A flawless porcelain face was framed by a coronet of hair the color of cornsilk; a white circlet atop her head was a halo. The dress was white silk shot with gold thread, and softly feathered wings flowed from the center of her back, the tips nearly reaching the hem of the dress. It was a work of art—a family heirloom.

"Do you want to do the honors?" he asked.

"Oh, I couldn't." She put up her hands. "That's gorgeous, Blake."

"It's been in the family a long time."

"It's your tree," she said. "You should be the one to put it on."

Blake disappeared to the kitchen and came back with a step stool. He put it on the floor and held out the angel. "It's your tree, too," he said.

"Blake…"

"Please?"

Her hands trembled as she took the delicate figure from his hands and stepped up on the stool. He stood beside her, and she was acutely aware of his shoulder next to her rib cage as she leaned forward and carefully placed the angel over the top bough of the tree. The cone inside the skirt slid over the pointed top and settled firmly into place as Hope let out the breath she'd been holding and turned around.

The step stool put her higher than Blake, so that his face was just below hers. He was standing close…so close she could feel the warmth of his body, smell the faint spiciness of his aftershave.

"Perfect," he whispered.

He wasn't looking at the tree. He was looking at her. Gazing into her eyes with his own deep blue ones.

She felt herself going, losing what was left of her common sense in the depths of them. Before she could think better of it she lifted her hand and laid it along his cheek— the one with the scar. She ran her finger down the length of it slowly, carefully, her heart breaking at the difference in texture of the scar tissue, its smoothness oddly perfect when its very presence was a symbol of such pain and loss.

His hands spanned her ribs and lifted her from the stool, put her feet firmly on the floor.

And once she was steady he took her hand from his face, squeezed her fingers and kissed her.

CHAPTER SEVEN

"Perfect," Blake had heard himself say. But he couldn't drag his gaze away from her.

The way she was looking at him made it impossible. He'd never talked about Brad like that before—not to anyone but his parents. It made people uncomfortable. But not Hope. She'd spoken in such a matter-of-fact way that it had been a relief to express how he missed his brother.

And then she did the last thing he expected. She rested her hand on his scar, tracing the length of it with warm, soft fingertips. Exploring. Caressing.

He spanned her waist and lifted her down, never taking his gaze off hers. She wasn't backing away this time. The music played softly and the lights glowed around them. And right now all he wanted to do was feel close to someone. To her. He knew in his heart that this could never truly go anywhere, but what she'd given him broke down all his resolve. With nothing more than a touch she'd accepted him, scar and all.

He covered her hand with his, pulled it away and squeezed her fingers—the fingers that had given him back something he'd lost long ago: faith. Faith that someone would see past the scar and see who he really was. Inside, where it mattered.

He dipped his head and kissed her lips. Warm,

cinnamon-spicy lips that opened beneath his and for one breathless moment made him believe that anything was possible.

All Hope's senses were on full alert as Blake touched his lips to hers. The glow of the Christmas lights beside them. The scent of the tree and mulling spice in the air. The sound of Christmas songs on the television. It was the kind of holiday moment she saw in the movies and read about in books; the kind that never happened to a girl like her but kept her up late on Christmas Eve under a blanket, with a DVD, a box of tissues beside her glass of wine and a packet of store-bought shortbreads that were never quite as good as Gram's.

But here she was, closing her eyes as Blake's warm lips beguiled her, tasting of cider and something far more potent than the tot of rum she'd put in his mug. His arm slipped around her, drawing her closer, and she put her hand on his shoulder, feeling the exciting firmness of his muscles beneath her fingers. He drew back slightly, their breaths mingling in the charged silence as the song switched. She bit down on her lip and chanced a look up at him, desperately wanting more and terribly afraid he might just realize it.

Looking up was a mistake and a blessing. The first petals of curiosity had been plucked and had been replaced by the more exotic bloom of desire and need. Blake's embrace tightened and Hope wrapped her arms around his neck as their mouths met again, hotter, more demanding. Her breasts were crushed against his shirtfront and his wide palm pressed against the curve of her back, molding their bodies together as their breathing quickened.

She hadn't expected this explosion, this powerful craving for him. It would only take a word and they'd be in bed together. Hope knew it, and the thought made her blood race. It would be fantastic. Blake was the kind of man who would be gentle and physical all at once. Careful, yet thorough. Sexy, yet loving.

And that last was what made Hope hesitate, back away from the heat of his touch and the glory of his mouth.

This wouldn't be a casual one-nighter. A brief encounter with no strings. Blake wasn't that kind of man.

And she wasn't that kind of woman either. She wouldn't be able to simply get up and walk away.

The alternative was getting in way too deep…or backing off.

She gathered all her fortitude and took another step backward, nearly tripping over the step stool, righting herself while her cheeks flamed and her heart seemed to pound a mile a minute.

"Hope…"

"Don't," she whispered, her voice hoarse. "We can't do this, okay?"

"You're afraid?"

Damn straight she was. Afraid of everything she was feeling lately. Afraid of getting caught up in holiday nostalgia. And most of all afraid of getting caught up in *him*. It would be so easy.

"I'm here for a few more days and then I'm gone. I don't do temporary flings, Blake. I'm not built that way."

"What *do* you do? Because it's perfectly clear that you don't do serious or commitment either. What's holding you back, Hope?"

Panic threaded through her limbs. "I'm just here to take pictures, okay?"

"Liar," he said softly, taking a step forward. "Those pictures are just a reason our grandmothers gave us both. Surely you'd figured that out by now?"

The very idea frightened her to death. "Are you saying you're…?" She choked on the next words. "On board with this? That you planned…?"

Oh, Lord. She was really starting to freak out now. Blake was looking at her in his strong and steady way, and she felt like a baby bird flapping its wings and still falling steadily toward the ground, waiting for the inevitable thud.

"Of course I didn't plan it. When you arrived I knew you were the last person I'd be interested in."

Ouch. That smarted. Even if it was what she wanted to hear, it stung just the same.

"Ditto," she replied.

"And now we have this." He swept out his hand. "It would appear we weren't quite as right as we would have liked to believe."

"It…it was just a kiss," she stammered.

"Yes, it was." He came closer and put his hands on her upper arms. "So why all the panic?"

"Because… Because…" But she couldn't form the words for a coherent explanation.

Because she didn't do emotional intimacy. And here she was, talking about it with him. Here she was, at his place, wiping away tears as she watched a young boy hug a horse or listened to the laughter of a girl who had very little to laugh about. This whole place was opening her up to a world of pain she'd shut the door on years ago. It was getting harder and harder to pack those feelings back into the box where they belonged. And what terrified her most was that she was afraid there would come a time that she couldn't, and then she'd break.

"I know."

His deep voice slid over her soul. He really did know, didn't he? It was in his eyes when he looked at the photo of his brother. It was in his smile when he lifted Cate from her pony or sent Anna home with the little bit extra left over from dinner. He didn't seem the least bit afraid of caring. But he knew she was. Because he'd been there.

She hadn't truly cried in years, but right now tears threatened as everything—past, present, future—seemed to overwhelm her. It was like she was standing at a crossroads and it was too painful to go back, too frightening to move forward, but impossible to stay where she was.

She'd never felt more alone.

"What do you want from me, Blake?"

There was a long pause. "Nothing."

"It doesn't feel like nothing. *That* didn't feel like nothing." She lifted her chin, challenging. "Do you want to sleep with me?" she pushed. "Or was it just a kiss? Out of the blue, perhaps? Maybe you just got caught up in the moment? Or were you looking for something more from a poor confused girl who needs fixing?"

He ran a hand over his hair. "Dammit, Hope, I don't know!"

The words rang out, followed by a crystal clear silence between them.

"No, you don't," she said quietly. "And it's unfair to take things further when neither of us knows what we want."

"Why did you touch me, then?"

He turned the tables and butterflies started winging their way through her stomach again. She could still feel the texture of the skin on his cheek, marveled at the strength of him and the vulnerability, too.

She ignored the question. "Blake, we both know this is a mistake. Let's just chalk it up to some spiced rum and holiday spirit and leave it at that. There's no sense complicating it with things that will never be, and we both know it."

"So reasonable," he replied, his eyes blazing.

"I don't want to get hurt," she answered.

"You think you could?" He took a step closer.

"I might," she admitted.

He didn't know how many feelings had truly come to the surface during this trip. Didn't know how many barriers he'd broken down simply by being himself. He could *never* know that.

Shaken, she looked up at him. "I need some time. A little while to…"

He nodded. "Fine. I'll clean up here."

"You're sure?"

His eyes seemed to see everything, to see right through to the heart of her as he nodded. "I'm sure. You go on."

She turned and fled the room, heading for her bedroom.

When she got there she closed the door carefully and sat on the bed. She bit down on her lip. Longings she hadn't allowed herself for years had surfaced, all resurrected by the power of his kiss. She'd felt beautiful, cherished, strong and capable of anything. But now it was over she was faced with the truth. She was an emotional wreck. She didn't know how to love, didn't know how to trust anyone. She'd failed so many times to hold her family together. She'd wanted so many things for them all and instead they'd ended up at opposite ends of the globe. Her mother, father, Faith, Grace…all spread out.

She remembered Gram's weary words the day she'd finally given up.

"You can't take the happiness of so many on your own shoulders," Gram had said wisely. "It's okay, Hope. You can let it go."

She'd let go of the responsibility, but she'd let go of her family, too.

And she missed them. Despite their differences and distance, she missed them.

She dried her tears and blew her nose. She had to stop thinking about Blake and put things in perspective. A few days from now and she'd be in Beckett's Run.

She decided to forget about long distance and roaming charges and dialed Faith's number. She needed a sister, and in her fragile state she wanted Faith, who had always been the gentlest of the three of them. Faith, who would be easier to talk to than Grace right now.

"Hello?" came a sleepy voice after the fourth ring.

"Crikey, I forgot about the time difference." Hope calculated in her head and realized that it was nearly midnight in England.

"Hope?" Incredulity colored her sister's voice.

"I really am sorry, Faith. Go back to sleep."

"I wasn't asleep." There was a sigh from the other end. "Is everything okay?"

"How did you know it was me?" Hope lay down on the bed, sinking into the pillows.

"I don't know many people who say 'crikey' in an American accent."

"Right…"

"Are you okay, Hope?" Faith's normally gentle voice held a note of worry. "You *never* call. And you sound…" She paused. "Is Gram okay?"

That was part of the problem, wasn't it? She never called. And now that Hope had her sister on the phone, she didn't know what to say.

"Gram's okay and so am I."

"Well, that's a relief."

Hope sighed and leaned back on the pillows. "I was just wondering… Does it strike you funny that Gram has asked all three of us to do favors for old friends? I mean, me with the photos, you and the stained glass—and Gram said Grace is going back to Beckett's Run…"

"I don't follow."

"Well…" Hope brushed her hand over her eyes. "I mean right smack in the middle of all three are…"

"Men?"

There was an acerbic tone to Faith's voice that made Hope sit up. *"Yes,"* she said emphatically. "You know Grace is going to see J.C. when she's back? And this Marcus guy, for example…what's his deal?"

"You mean *Lord* Westerham?" Faith huffed out a sigh. "He's a thorn in my side, that's all."

"I hear that," Hope replied, sitting cross-legged in the middle of the bed. "Blake is driving me crazy."

"Crazy good?"

Now, *that* was a loaded question. "Truthfully?"

"I could use a diversion. What happened?"

"We kissed. That's all."

She could nearly hear Faith's smile through the phone. "You kissed? That's all?"

"That's what I said."

"You didn't sleep with him?"

"Faith!"

Faith's soft laugh echoed in Hope's ear. "All this fuss over a kiss? Imagine what Grace would say."

The unstoppable Grace always took life by the tail and never angsted over a simple kiss, did she?

And in that moment Hope realized something strange and important. She envied her youngest sister. She admired her. Grace had never been burdened by the responsibility of keeping the family together. It showed in the way she lived her life—on her terms and with no apologies. Grace, of all of them, was the most courageous.

Hope had never been that brave. And it showed.

"Hope? You still there?"

"I'm here."

Faith's voice was serious again. "Are you okay, really? You never call like this."

"I just got to thinking about when we were kids and stuff. We had some good times, right? Especially at Gram's. I was pretty put off by being told I had to go home for Christmas, but I'm sort of looking forward to it now. How about you?"

There was a pause, and then Faith sighed again. "Hope, there's something you should know before you fly home."

Alarm bells started ringing in Hope's head. "What is it?"

"It's Mom. It seems she…and Dad are both in Beckett's Run for the holidays."

Hope didn't miss the pause before the word *dad*. It had always been really hard for Faith once she'd found out that she had a different father from her two sisters. It had been the nail in the coffin of her parents' marriage, really. The moment that their father—Greg—had finally had enough.

"That must be tense," she managed to say.

"Apparently not as tense as you'd think."

Faith's voice held an implication that was startling. Hope sat back and let that tidbit of news sink in. Their parents were actually getting along?

"I'm glad you called," Faith continued. "This way you've got a heads up."

The line was silent for a moment or two. Did Hope want to open the Pandora's Box that was their relationship with their parents? She closed her eyes and pressed her hand to her forehead. Not tonight. It was too complicated. They'd be on the phone for hours.

"Does Grace know?"

"I don't know."

Another telling pause. Hope wondered what Faith thought of it all. And Grace… The three girls were so different. But they all bore the scars of their inconsistent childhood in their own way.

"Faith, listen. I just wanted to call and say…" Say what, exactly? It was going to sound stupid and emotional, and that wasn't Hope's style.

"Say what, Hope?"

"That I'm sorry. I gave up on the family and I shouldn't have. I wish we'd stayed closer, you know? We're sisters." She thought of Blake and Brad. They wouldn't have another chance. But Hope did.

"You tried too hard, that's all." Faith's voice was warm and reassuring. "You tried to step into Mom's shoes and we resented you for it."

"Not you. You were never as hard to handle as Grace."

"I just handled it differently. I quit playing peacemaker and walked away. I'm as much to blame as you, Hope."

Hope's lower lip trembled as the simple words of truth touched her heart. "I think it's going to be good to see you this Christmas."

Faith laughed. "Me, too. Goodness, I don't know who this Blake guy is, but he must be something to bring all this about."

A hot flush seemed to crawl up Hope's body. Something? Oh, he was something all right. Not that she would go into details.

"He just makes me think, that's all."

"Right. So what's the problem? Why not see what happens? When was the last time you were involved with someone?"

The answer to that was long and complicated. She gave her sister the short version. "I'm flying out in a few days. I hardly know him. The only alternatives are to drop everything in Sydney to be with him, or try a long-distance thing from Australia to Canada. Based on what? Ten days? Either option would be crazy." No matter how great a kisser he was.

"You're right. That doesn't sound very practical. And you're not the risk-taker in the family."

Hope let out a breath. "See? You *get* it. What about you and the Earl?"

"Oh, no," Faith replied. "You called *me*. We're talking about you. Not me."

"For now."

"You should go. This has to be costing you a small fortune."

Hope recognized a diversion when she heard it, but things were going too well for her to persist and risk the fragile connection they'd made. "It is, but I'm glad I called. I'll see you in a few days, yeah?"

"You got it."

"Bye, Faith." She hit the end button and put the phone on the night table.

It had been right to call. Right to reconnect. And it had felt good to put into words how she'd been feeling about Blake. No matter how attracted she was becoming, no matter how much she was drawn into caring for him, anything more was a ridiculous idea doomed to disaster. Look at her parents. They'd dated briefly and jumped right into marriage and they'd *all* paid for that mistake. The very idea that both of them were in Beckett's Run now, making nice, made Hope roll her eyes. Why would this time be any different than before? She hoped Faith wasn't getting her hopes up for some big reconciliation. Hope was sure that this time would be exactly the same as all the others.

It was insane to think of anything coming of her time here with Blake. Anything serious was inconceivable in this short amount of time. And anything else was just pointless, wasn't it?

And there was still his Christmas party to get through.

She was just going to have to toughen up and Scrooge her way through—to keep them both from being hurt in the end.

Blake turned his head at the sound of heels on the concrete of the barn floor. His first appointment wasn't due for another half hour, and he knew that particular sound anyway. Hope's heeled boots—the silly ones she'd worn the first day and that he'd hoped she'd wear again each day since. Totally impractical, yes. Also totally sexy.

He stepped out of the stall, stood the shovel on its end and rested his arms against the handle.

"You're up early."

"Just wanted to let you know I'll be gone for the day. I don't have a present for Gram or my sisters, and the last thing I want to be doing is shopping at the airport."

"Nothing says love like an airport gift shop."

She smiled. She had on that red puffy jacket again— the one that made her cheeks look extra rosy.

"Exactly. Even worse would be the shops in Beckett's Run on Christmas Eve, after everything's been picked over."

Never mind that he understood exactly what she was doing. Putting distance between them. Things had been strained ever since that kiss, despite their attempts to keep it casual and pleasant. There was an *atmosphere* now.

But he wasn't going to do anything to stop her. She'd brought him up short the other night, asking him what he wanted from her. He didn't have an answer. He wanted her. He wanted to feel close to her. But beyond that she was absolutely right. She was leaving in a few days. A rough-

and-ready tumble in the hay might be on his mind, but it wouldn't help matters any—not in the long run.

And it was probably better if she was out of his hair for the day. Being so close to her, smelling her shampoo in the moist heat of the bathroom after her shower, the hint of lipstick on the edge of a coffee cup...

Everything about her was driving him crazy. In all the very best and worst ways.

"Drive carefully and enjoy yourself," he advised, keeping a bland expression on his face.

She looked at him strangely but smiled, shifting her purse over her shoulder. "I will."

Her boots clicked over the concrete once more and he resumed shoveling.

But damned if he could get her out of his mind, or decide what he was going to do about it.

Hope headed toward the downtown core of Calgary, hoping to get there early and finish before lunch. There was one place in particular she needed to stop on the way home and it was quite a bit out of the way. She had found the perfect present for Blake. One that he'd never see coming. She couldn't keep herself from imagining the look on his face when she presented him with bells for his sleigh. It had taken some searching but she'd found them.

And if it looked like he was going to make too much of it, she'd say they were for Cate. It had been the little girl, after all, who had looked up at him with huge, innocent eyes and insisted that the sleigh have a set of bells.

She parked and wrapped her scarf around her neck, enjoying the walk through the bustling streets. It felt familiar, the crush of people going to work, cell phones pressed to ears and random conversations happening all around her. It was vital. It was teeming with life.

Then she thought about standing on the crest of the ridge with Blake, looking out over the mountains. That was vital, too. And awesome. A place where a person could be quiet with their own thoughts.

She stopped at an intersection and waited for the light to change. Frowning, she stared at the flashing orange hand. Had all the noise of her life kept her from thinking too much?

The light changed and she hotfooted it across the street surrounded by men and women, all headed to their destinations. Where was she headed? She hardly knew anymore. But she rather suspected that her old way of living wasn't going to fit quite the same way again. And where did that leave her?

Stephen Avenue Walk was awash in holiday spirit. Banners hung from old-fashioned-looking light posts, and above her head Christmas lights were strung across the walk. No vehicles were permitted on the street so pedestrians mingled freely. In front of one store she marveled at an intricately carved ice sculpture of a Christmas tree and presents. Each storefront was draped in ribbons and bows and sparkled with red and green and gold. She could only imagine what it would look like at night, all lit up, and could almost see herself wandering along with a gingerbread latte in hand.

And someone to share it with.

She took her camera out of her handbag and snapped a few pictures. It wasn't good that she was imagining strolling through the walk with Blake, holding hands and admiring the decorations, doing some last-minute shopping. She tucked her camera away and zipped up her bag. She was here to shop for her family, and that was what she was going to do.

Venturing on, she entered an upscale shopping center.

At a bookstore she found a hardcover book featuring a beautiful stained-glass collection. She bought a stunning cashmere scarf and glove set in the department store for Gram, wincing at the price tag but wanting to treat her grandmother to something fancy and upscale.

She browsed through the store, admiring the fine clothes and gazing at perfume bottles with longing. But today wasn't for her. She resisted the urge to treat herself even as she passed the lingerie section. She had a weakness for pretty underwear and nearly gave in when she spotted an emerald-green silk bra and panty set on sale. But she turned away, knowing she didn't need it. Knowing that there weren't any occasions to warrant it in her future.

And yet she hesitated, just for a heartbeat, remembering the look in Blake's eyes as he'd kissed her. There could be, couldn't there? If she allowed it. If she let him in.

Getting away for the day had been smart. Even this morning, in the barn, there'd been a light in his eyes that was hard to resist.

In the end she gave it one last longing glance and moved on.

She still had to find something for Grace—the hardest present of all. What could she get for a woman who didn't settle down? Who lived her life from a suitcase? Perhaps Faith and Hope lived oceans apart, but they'd made lives for themselves in one place. Grace traveled endlessly.

At a gallery she spent more than she'd planned on a small painting for Grace—a grove of trees leading to a river. It reminded Hope of summer days in Beckett's Run. The colors were soft and blended, giving it a lazy, nostalgic feeling. Looking at it, she felt her throat tighten. Her sisters hadn't given up on her, had they? She'd given up on them. Or, more accurately, she'd given up on herself.

It was too late now to get those years back. Grace in particular was angry with her, and rightfully so.

Before she could change her mind, she handed over her credit card and bought the piece. Grace traveled, but she did still have an apartment. A home base. Maybe the girls couldn't go back to those days, but if they were all going to be together for Christmas perhaps they could remember some good times.

With her sisters and grandmother taken care of, that just left Blake. As Hope wandered farther into the historic district she saw a store boasting Westernwear. Unable to resist, she went inside.

It smelled of leather and cotton, and Hope couldn't hold back the small smile that touched her lips. This was Blake's world, wasn't it? Boots and leather, jeans and belt buckles. She didn't know why she was here, really—her plan had been to pick up the sleigh bells and that was it. But there wasn't anything wrong with getting him a small something to say thank you, was there? After all she'd been staying in his house and eating his food for more than a week already.

And she was giving him plenty in return—professional photos, a part of her argued.

She ignored the thought. She could buy someone a present if she wanted. She ran her fingers over the soft fabric of a red long-sleeved shirt. Blake looked good in red. It set off his complexion and made the blue of his eyes stand out somehow. Kind of like it had just before he'd kissed her in front of the Christmas tree.

She swallowed. It was just a shirt, right?

And she really should get something for Anna, she justified. After all, Blake was her host but Anna cared for the house and did most of the cooking. That was all these things were—host and hostess gifts. Nothing deeper than that. She found a silver hair clip set with turquoise that was gorgeous, and added it to her purchases.

Ten minutes later she walked out, hands full of shopping bags and well satisfied with the morning's work. A quick stop at another department store secured wrapping paper and bows. She was all set now, wasn't she? To her surprise she found she was actually excited for the holiday—something that hadn't happened in years.

Her stomach growled, so she stopped for a sandwich and a coffee and opted to eat outside. It was cool, but not cold; she took her simple lunch to Olympic Plaza and sat, enjoying the sight of skaters swirling around what was a wading pool in summer, and admiring the arches built for medal presentations during a previous winter Olympics. She sipped her coffee and sighed. She liked it here. It was a big city, with big oil and gas money, but there was still a feeling about it—a down-to-earthness that she appreciated. She'd bet this place was beautiful in the summertime.

And the mountains were only an hour away.

And so was Blake.

Disturbed at the direction of her thoughts, she threw her wrapper and cup in a garbage can and made her way back to the parking lot. She still had to drive to the southwest corner of the city to pick up the bells, and then make her way back to Bighorn before dinner.

As she brought up the address on her GPS she frowned. She'd taken a day away from the ranch to get away from Blake, to stop thinking about him. And instead he'd been in her thoughts all morning. More than in her thoughts.

He'd been everywhere. And it was more than just appreciating the sight of him in well-fitting jeans and boots. It was inside. She cared for him. When he was with her it was like someone lit a candle inside her, warm and bright. She was falling for him, and that was *so* not the plan.

It was only the indisputable knowledge that nothing could come of it that kept her from moving forward, from exploring what might be between them. As she'd told Faith, the idea of a long-distance relationship was ludicrous, as was the notion that she'd leave everything behind in Sydney without a hint of a guarantee.

She only had a few more days. If she and Blake gave in to temptation it would only make leaving more difficult, wouldn't it?

Hope headed south on Macleod Trail and let out a huge breath. She just had to get through this party thing, which shouldn't be too difficult, right? There would be plenty of people around running interference. She'd probably hardly even see Blake during all the ruckus.

And damned if that didn't make her feel even more lonely.

CHAPTER EIGHT

HOPE tried to stay out of Blake's way the next day. She
sorted some laundry and wrapped her presents, and waited
until she saw him walking across the yard to the barn before heading for the kitchen to scrounge some breakfast

She put her bowl and coffee mug in the dishwasher
before booting up her laptop. Today she was going to go
through the pictures she had and make a short list, then
start editing. Blake needed a good dozen images to use
in his brochure and on his website.

She frowned as she moved two unusable pictures of
Cate into her discard folder. Blake had more than one PR
problem. Hope could give him the best photos in the world
but his current website design wasn't doing him any favors. She wondered what his plans were. He could do with
a redesign. Something that captured the feel of the place
and the program rather than a standard template straigh
from a hosting package. She knew of several people who
had the know-how to set it up, and then it would merely
be a matter of updating; something Hope, even with he
basic skills, could show him.

Except she wasn't going to be here, was she? And she'd
guess that Blake would find it hard to take money from
his budget to hire a web designer. Which left him with
his basic site.

It was past noon when Hope lifted her head and rubbed her eyes. She gazed absently out the living room window and saw Blake walking back and forth with a gigantic snow scoop. Curious, she went to the window. She could see now. He was clearing a large patch of ice. With the snow removed Hope could see that the rink was bordered by planks, forming a perimeter. He put the scoop aside and brushed off two huge logs beside the rink. Seats? She smiled to herself. Benches?

His hat was pulled low over his head, his breath making frosty clouds in the air as he picked up shovel and scoop together and headed back to the barn. She swallowed. She couldn't deny—at least to herself—that she found his strength and physicality incredibly attractive. She'd never considered herself a fan of the big, rugged outdoorsy type, but Blake's roughness was what made him different, made him stand out. Paired with what she knew now was a gentle heart... Well, it made a devastating combination.

She managed to keep a grip on her hormones when he came in for lunch. Anna had fixed her a sandwich. She ate sitting at her laptop and then went to change her laundry over to the dryer while Blake ate his standing at the counter.

"Sorry to rush," he said between mouthfuls. "The guys will be here anytime."

"The guys?"

"Weekly game. We usually have it on a Sunday, but now that high school's out for the holidays we planned it today. Anna's son, John, comes over and captains the other team, and a bunch of local teenagers keep us on our toes. You can come and watch if you want." He waggled his eyebrows. "Be a puck bunny."

He seemed to be oblivious to everything that had happened before. The long looks, the dim lights, the way they'd kissed next to the Christmas tree. It was like nothing had ever happened between them, and on one hand she was relieved and on the other annoyed. The least he could do was show a bit of the awkwardness that *she* was feeling when they were in the same room together. But there was nothing. He was completely at ease.

She blinked and stared at her monitor without really seeing. Maybe *she* was the one making too big a deal out of everything. Maybe she was the only one who stared at the ceiling at night, unable to go to sleep, knowing he was just down the hall. She'd asked him what he wanted from her and he'd said nothing. Maybe he was right and she was making a mountain out of a molehill.

She ignored the puck bunny reference deliberately. "I really should keep working. I only have a few more days to get this sorted for you." She looked at him out of the corner of her eye. Part of his figure was obscured by the frame of her reading glasses.

He shrugged. "Suit yourself."

He went out the door minutes later and Hope let out a breath. Shortly after she heard the low drone of a snowmobile go past the house, and then a few trucks pulled into the yard. Her concentration shot, she watched curiously as nets were set up at either end of the rink and a line of boys—men, rather, looking at their size—sat on the logs, lacing up skates and putting on helmets.

One by one they stepped onto the ice, sticks riding close to the surface. A puck appeared and there was some passing back and forth, and shooting at the empty nets. Two players shuffled onto the ice in full goalie gear—pads, mask, glove and blocker. They smacked their sticks on the ice in a testosterone-fueled show of hubris as they began making practice saves.

And then the disorganized scrimmaging became a game.

It was easy to tell Blake from the others. He stood a good three inches taller than anyone else on the ice, and he moved the puck with a grace and finesse that the other players lacked. For the first few minutes he didn't get a chance at the net: a pass was intercepted, and a poke check turned over the puck. But then she saw it…the opening. And Blake did, too. With fast feet he zoomed up the ice, let the puck sit on his stick, before flicking his wrist and sending it flying—straight over the glove of the goalie and into the mesh at the back of the net.

Hope let out the breath she'd been holding and laughed. She hadn't watched hockey in years, but spending time in Massachusetts meant that she'd watched her share of Bruins games. She knew enough about the sport to appreciate the players below.

A few congratulatory slaps from his teammates and they were off again. Hope looked over at her computer and then at her camera, sitting in its bag at the end of the table. She couldn't resist.

Within five minutes she'd dressed in heavy coat, hat and boots and made her way toward the ice, camera dangling around her neck. She waded through the snow to the edge of the fence—Blake wouldn't see her here unless he was looking, but she had a clear view and could zoom in to capture everything she needed.

She took pictures for over an hour. Pictures of the men swooping and swirling on the ice. Pictures of sticks raised in victory after a goal. Of Blake, his long legs extended as he raced for the puck, his arms lifted as he released the puck, and—the best one of all—Blake laughing. His eyes sparkled blue fire and his mouth was open as he laughed, his cheeks ruddy with color beneath the black helmet.

She could hear the glorious sound of it across the

snowy field and it warmed her from the inside out. She found herself smiling in response. Blake's laugh made her happy, she realized. And she also realized that while she'd shed tears this past week she'd also laughed more, smiled more—more than she had in a really long time.

She felt alive here.

And she was going to miss it when she left.

That was the biggest surprise of all. Never in her life had she lived in a place this isolated. She couldn't even see another house from here. It was a long drive just to the nearest convenience store, and almost an hour to the closest city when she was used to everything being within a few blocks. But it had little to do with the place. It was bigger than that. It was Blake, and the simple acceptance he offered toward everyone who passed through the gates.

She didn't have to pretend to be anyone she wasn't when she was here, and it had made the pressure inside her seep away. She couldn't remember ever feeling this relaxed, without the weight of expectation and responsibility on her head. Being here, with Blake, had made her want things she hadn't wanted in a very long time.

The game wound up and she continued taking pictures. There was one she knew she was going to like—six huge male bodies, their backs to her, sitting on a log taking off their skates. Their voices mingled in the crisp air. And then she was sure one of them caught sight of her. She paused, her heart seizing, as he elbowed Blake and nodded in her direction.

She didn't need to zoom in to know that Blake's gaze had found her. His teeth flashed as he smiled, and he picked up the bag that held his gear.

Then he started walking toward her.

His stride was long and purposeful and as he drew closer Hope could make out the impish smile on his face and…oh, yes. A glint in his eye. He dropped his bag and catcalls echoed out behind them. Intuition told her she was in trouble, and she hurried to zip her camera back into the vinyl case sitting on the snow beside her.

"Taking pictures, are we?"

His voice was deep and rich, and it sent tingles down her spine it was so delicious.

She lifted her chin even as she continued walking backward. "Isn't that my job?"

Blake scooped up some snow, molded it in his hands, and kept walking.

"Did you get everyone to sign a release?" he teased, his steps menacing as he drew closer.

"D-don't," she stammered, stumbling backward and feeling the oddest temptation to burst out laughing.

A snowball fight? Just when she thought she had him figured out he came up with another surprise. His sense of humor was definitely suited for children…

"I mean it, Blake!" She would *not* engage in a silly snowball fight.

The first snowball hit her in the arm.

She bent down to grab her own snow and quickly pressed it into a ball—she had to defend herself, after all!

"Blake…"

He had more snow in his hand. She drew back and let her snowball fly, needing the distraction so she could get away. The ball just grazed the top of his head and he laughed, letting go with another and hitting her square in the chest. A clump of thick snow clung to her zipper. She stared at it for a millisecond before throwing another, missing him completely. As she bent for more snow he ran through the white fluff and captured her, circling her with his arms before she could throw the next one.

She struggled against his embrace, losing the battle

against laughter. "Let me go, you big goon!" she gasped, throwing out her elbows. But it was no use. He was laughing, too, and not even close to letting her go.

"You show 'er, Blake!" came a call from behind them.

Hope's mind raced, searching for a strategy to get free.

She looped one foot around the back of his boot, stopped struggling long enough to place her hands on his chest—and shoved.

Blake toppled over like a felled tree, just as she'd planned. But he grabbed her jacket and pulled her over with him—not what she'd planned at all.

They hit the ground in a mass of tangled legs and arms, with Hope most definitely sprawled on top of him in a most undignified manner, her face inches from his as the other hockey players let out whoops and cries.

Time seemed to hold still for several seconds as she looked down into his eyes. "Blake…" she warned, but it only added fuel to the fire.

"I'm sorry, Hope," he murmured. "I can't help it." And then he lifted his right hand, cupped the back of her hat, and pulled her head down until he was kissing her.

His lips and nose were cold, but his mouth was warm as he held her head in place. She knew she shouldn't—not after the other day, not after she'd decided there'd be no more flirting or intimate moments. But she couldn't resist his kiss and she let herself go, let herself enjoy the feel and taste of him. She reveled in the sound of his breath in the winter stillness, loved how the kiss teased and played.

He shifted his weight and suddenly she found herself beneath him, pressed into snow that was sharp and cold and yet somehow insulating.

"I've wanted to do that since the other day," he murmured. "Told myself I wouldn't. You make it hard on a man, Hope McKinnon."

He wasn't kissing her now. He was just looking at her, and she was looking at him. She couldn't seem to stop gazing into his eyes. And just when she wondered if he was going to let her up, he lowered his head again and made her go all soft and swoony by using his lips in a very effective manner. She didn't stop him. It felt too perfect, too wonderful. The flame inside her that he seemed to kindle so easily flickered to life. When he looked at her this way, kissed her this way, she felt alive. Beautiful. Cherished. Like anything was possible.

She was dimly aware of the sound of vehicle doors slamming, engines starting and trucks disappearing, and still they went on kissing. Soft kisses, light kisses, deep and passionate kisses. His body was heavy and warm as it pressed against her and she shifted the tiniest bit. Blake groaned into her mouth and a surge of feminine power raced through her veins.

She and Blake could take this inside. It would take very little convincing to move this to a warmer location with fewer clothes.

And it would be spectacular. She knew that instinctively.

Everywhere he was touching her now—even through clothing—felt like it was on fire. Blake would be gentle and thorough and intense. The blaze of desire flared inside her. All it would take was the right word.

The right word and he could be hers.

But was that really what she wanted? For the next hour, *yes*. Absolutely. His lips touched her neck and she struggled to breathe. But what about after that?

It always came back to the same thing. She stilled beneath him and he lifted his head. He was so beautiful, she realized, scar or not. It was more than that. It was how the man inside shone through his eyes and the set of his jaw.

She blinked against the moisture that gathered in the corners of her eyes. She cared too much. It wasn't love—it couldn't be and she knew that. But there was a connection between the two of them—perhaps there had been from the moment he'd offered her his hand when she'd fallen on the ice. He'd broken through the wall she normally kept around her heart like it had never even been there.

And she hadn't seen him coming.

His gaze deepened and he kissed each eyelid with such tenderness she thought she might fall apart right there in his arms.

"What is it?" he murmured the words in the silence. "Tell me, Hope."

How could she explain it without making herself even more vulnerable? "I can't do this," she whispered.

His eyes smiled down at her. "We can move it inside. I'm pretty sure Anna's gone home by now."

"That's not what I meant," she began.

The gaze that had been gently teasing before now sharpened hungrily. "I want to be with you," he answered. "Really be with you. Even if it's just this one time. I've never met anyone like you."

Oh, glory. If only he knew how much she wanted to say yes. He wasn't making it any easier. But then nothing was easy with Blake.

In the end, her need for self-preservation won out.

"It would be a mistake. We'd both regret it, Blake." She bit down on her lip, because even as she said it she was thinking about kissing him again.

Her legs and bottom were getting numb from the cold snow, she realized. She should get up and walk away. But she couldn't make herself push him away. Not yet.

"Why?" he asked. He shifted one leg so it rubbed up

against hers. "We've got means, motive and definitely opportunity."

Why did he have to be so charming?

He brushed his lips over the crest of her cheek, his breath warm as it slid over her skin.

"We're both grown-ups," he continued, sprinkling kisses over her face, little flecks of heat in contrast to the chill. "Both consenting adults. With a house to ourselves." He added the last with special significance.

All good reasons on the "for" side.

But it really only took one good "against" to throw a kink into the works.

"I can't be casual about this," she answered, wishing for the first time ever that she could be more free and easy about things rather than take everything to heart. "I'm leaving, remember?"

"You don't exactly let me forget it."

"Blake, I don't bounce back easily." She put her hands on either side of his face and forced his head around so that she could look him square in the face. She knew she guarded herself closely, and as a result she could often seem like she didn't care, but the truth was she often cared too much. "If we do this it'll make leaving even worse, don't you see?"

"Because you have feelings?"

"Because I can't do this *without* feelings."

She gulped, wondering what he'd think if he knew how much it had cost her to be that honest. Wondered what he'd think if he understood exactly how inexperienced she was and that she didn't take sex lightly. There'd been one time at the end of high school, which had been a horrible, horrible mistake, and twice more—both in her twenties, both relationships that hadn't panned out. Instead they'd fizzled out before they'd ever had the chance to get serious.

His gaze cooled. "That's clear enough, then."

She suddenly realized that he'd misunderstood. She'd meant that she wasn't a woman who could be casual about sleeping with someone. It had always been more than physical gratification to her. She'd meant—God help her—that her feelings were already involved. But he'd taken it literally—presuming that she had no such feelings for him. He was so wrong. He had no idea how completely he held her in the palm of his hand. How close she was to breaking. How much he made her feel about everything.

She wished she could explain, but she couldn't possibly open up about her real feelings. She didn't know how to have a holiday romance and still leave with herself intact at the end.

He pushed himself off of her and, just like the first time they'd met, offered his hand to help her up. She took it, feeling a mixture of relief and regret, and definitely unsatisfied in the most primal, physical sense.

"Blake, please understand." She tipped up her face and on impulse peeled off her glove and put her hand to his cold cheek. "It is going to hurt enough when I have to leave on Sunday. This would only make it hurt more."

"Why should it hurt?"

And there he was—still pushing her emotionally. He wanted her to say the words and it was unfair. It made her feel naked, with no defenses.

"Don't make me say it, okay?" There was a lump in her throat. "Isn't it enough that I've said this much?"

The air between them hummed with the words she hadn't said but they both knew.

"You can't keep kissing me like this. We need to keep it businesslike from now on." She didn't dare tell him that it was a very real possibility that he would wear her down.

A girl could only hold out for so long—especially when a giant part of her wanted to give in.

"Businesslike?"

She nodded. "If you care about me at all, please do as I ask," she said, hoping to appeal to his sense of honor.

His brow wrinkled and he reluctantly gave in. "All right," he replied. "No more kissing in the snowbanks."

"Or anywhere else," she cautioned.

"Or anywhere else," he confirmed.

"Thanks," she said, and skirted around him to retrieve her camera case.

He picked up his bag and followed her to the house, and Hope was relieved. At least that was what she told herself. But she was also disappointed.

She really did have to get out of here—back to Sydney and real life. It was far less complicated and way less painful—just the way she liked it.

Too bad she'd got the funny feeling that it wouldn't be the same.

CHAPTER NINE

THE morning of the Christmas party Hope kept her lap-top packed away and helped Anna with the preparations.

There was to be hot cocoa for the kids and hot spiced cider for the adults, as well as cookies and treats. While Anna went to work making iced shortbread, Hope donned a red-and-green apron and began making an old family favorite—Gram's Chocolate Truffle Cookies.

She'd called for the recipe yesterday, and been shocked to hear that Grace was out doing something Christmassy with J. C. Carson. She'd wondered if J.C. would make it through the evening uninjured. She'd said nothing to Gram, though, who'd sounded satisfied at the whole thing. And neither of them had mentioned Hope's parents.

She melted chocolate and then went to work on the dough, beating the butter and sugar while Anna hummed along with "Frosty The Snowman" on the radio as she spread icing on shortbread bells and stars.

Hope was up to her wrists in dough when Blake strolled in, cheeks ruddy from the cold and a smile on his face. "I think the sleigh is ready to go," he said. "And what have we here?" His gaze traveled from Hope's feet to her face. "In an apron? Surprising fashion statement, Hope."

"Oh, I'm full of surprises," Hope responded, rolling a spoonful of dough into a ball and placing it on a cookie sheet. "My grandmother's Chocolate Truffle Cookies. To die for. Wait and see."

"Full of surprises, hmmm?" he speculated, snatching a cookie from Anna's freshly frosted tray. He bit into it and a smidgen of green icing remained on his lip.

Hope stared at it and swallowed. It would be tempting to remove it personally, but she'd sworn off that sort of thing and Anna was right there, after all.

"You've got a…" She pointed at her own lip and then watched, fascinated, as his tongue slipped out to swipe the sweet bit of frosting away.

"Thanks."

She shrugged, rolling another cookie, filling the sheet. "Actually, I have an early present for you. Let me slip these into the oven and set the timer."

"A present?"

She nodded, butterflies swirling around in her stomach. Why on earth was she nervous? But she was. She avoided his gaze as she washed her hands and dried them on a towel. "I'll be right back," she said to Anna, who merely nodded as she worked on piping a red outline on a star.

She only had ten minutes—enough time to give him the present, not enough for them to be alone together for too long.

She hoped.

Blake followed her down the hall and into her room—the first time he'd been inside it since that afternoon she'd arrived and he'd carried her bag upstairs. The bed was neatly made and her suitcase was nowhere to be seen. Her laptop sat closed on a side table, the mouse pad and mouse precisely lined up at a right angle beside it.

Her perfectionist streak manifesting itself again?

Clearly Hope was nervous. She could barely look at

him, and her shoulders were tense. He smiled a little as
he saw a smudge of cocoa on her apron. That had been a
total surprise. Hope always seemed so put together, so…
He wasn't sure how to explain it. Untouchable, perhaps.
Out of his league with her tall, elegant looks. Either way,
baking cookies in an apron made her look different. Put
them on the same level somehow.

Maybe she was starting to unbend just a little bit. He
hoped so. If anyone needed to unwind and let go of tension it was Hope. He only wished he knew what had her so
tied up in knots. It wasn't just her friend Julie. He understood that now. She needed to grieve, and not just for her
friend. But what? Why was she so demanding of herself?

She disappeared into the closet. She'd bought him a
Christmas present and that surprised him—especially
after the episode in the snow. She'd told him she didn't
have feelings for him. She was a damned liar, but he knew
she didn't *want* to have feelings for him and that essentially amounted to the same thing. Hands off. No matter
what he was feeling in return.

Trouble was, he didn't want her to go. He wanted her
to stay, to see if what was between them was real. For the
first time since he'd broken up with his ex he trusted a
woman to see beyond the surface. It had all changed the
day she'd touched his scar with a tenderness and rever-
ence that had humbled him.

He wasn't sure if he was in love with her or not, but he
wanted the opportunity to find out. And he couldn't do
that if she left for good tomorrow.

"I hope these are what you were looking for," she said,
coming out of the closet carrying a gift bag very carefully
as if what was inside was incredibly fragile.

He took the bag from her hands and heard a funny jingle. He opened the bag and peered inside. His heart gave

a little catch. He reached in and pulled out a leather strap. The clear sound of bells filled the room.

"Cate said she wanted bells on the sleigh, so…"

He looked in her eyes. In the bright sunlight of her bedroom they were stunningly blue, full of hope and uncertainty. It hit him then. The professional manner, the precision and perfection—it wasn't confidence. It was covering up a massive case of insecurity. Was she worried he wouldn't like them? That they wouldn't suit? There were so many more layers to Hope than he'd first thought. It touched him that she was so obviously trying to please him. That she'd bothered to find something so appropriate, so personal.

He slid the leather over his palm and smiled. "They're perfect, Hope. Where ever did you find them?"

"In an antique store just outside Calgary," she replied. "You're sure they'll work?"

"Oh, they'll work. They'll be perfect." He looked up and smiled. "Thank you, Hope. It was very thoughtful of you to go to the trouble."

She blushed. Color infused the crests of her cheeks much to Blake's delight. The more she let go of the veneer she protected herself with, the more he liked her. Right now, with a bit of flour across the breast of her apron, her hair in a ponytail and a glow to her cheek, she looked adorable.

Was he actually considering a relationship, then? It would be a mistake to think that way. No matter how much he was starting to care for her, he knew she would never be happy here. Their lives were so different, and his first priority was the program.

She was right. He probably shouldn't have kissed her. Too bad he couldn't quite muster up an appropriate amount of regret.

"You're welcome. I thought…I thought the kids would like them."

"They will. They'll make tonight perfect." She was looking at him so hopefully he knew he had to keep the mood light before he got himself in trouble yet again. "I have something for you, too."

Her eyes widened. "You do?"

He nodded. "Not a present as such… Well, hold on. I'll get it and explain."

He made a quick trip to his room and grabbed the shopping bag from his closet. There was no guarantee she would go for it, but he hoped she would. Hope needed to let her hair down and show some silliness. They needed to have fun, and he had to stop thinking about her in ways that would get him nowhere. Their kisses before had been surprising and spontaneous, but there was something more now. A gravity between them. He couldn't quite put his finger on when or how it had changed but there was something—something important and a little sad and slightly desperate in these last twenty-four hours before her departure.

Back in her room, he handed her the bag. "I'm dressing up as Santa tonight and handing out some small presents to the kids. I was kind of hoping you would help."

She opened the bag and stared at the contents. "This is…" She put the bag down on the bed and drew out a hat, green-and-red striped, with a bell on the end. "This is an elf hat."

"Santa needs an elf," he said lightly, but he wasn't encouraged when he saw her frown.

She pulled out the tunic and tights and his favorite bit—the shoes, curled up at the toes and with bells attached to the tips.

"You can't be serious."

"Hey, at least you don't have to stuff your costume with pillows and wear a scratchy beard," he remarked, forcing a chuckle.

"You do realize I was hired to take pictures?"

"I know that. I thought over the last few days that had changed into something more." He remembered hearing her laugh as he tackled her in the snow, the taste of her lips all the sweeter because she'd been a willing and equal participant. He took her hand. "I thought we were something more," he said quietly.

"You know that's impossible."

And yet there was a hint of longing in her voice that he didn't miss. "So we're not friends?"

She pulled her hand away. "I didn't think that was what you meant. I hadn't really thought about it," she said, but her gaze slid from his. She *had* thought about it. They both had—too much.

"Have you never done something silly? Something just for fun, Hope? Have you seen the look on a kid's face when he or she sits on Santa's lap? It's Christmas. I want to give them something awesome—there's not enough fun in their lives. And I want to give you something, too."

"What's that?" She put the costume back on the bed and faced him, her guard fully up and functional again.

"A memory," he said. "A good Christmas memory. Because I think you need one—desperately."

The guard slipped just a little as her eyes widened and he saw his chance.

"Trust me." He lifted his hand and touched her cheek with his finger. "Can you trust me for tonight, Hope?"

"I leave tomorrow, Blake."

"I know that. Believe me, I know." He wished he had more time. Time to get to know her better. Time to…

Aw, hell. Maybe it was better this way. He was already

getting too involved. Much more and she'd really be able to hurt him. He knew for a fact that she wouldn't be back. She'd go back to her life in Sydney and that would be that, wouldn't it? Girls like her didn't stay. They didn't settle.

But it didn't stop the wanting. Or the need to do this for her. For all of them.

"Trust me," he repeated. "Wear the costume. Be my elf. Drink hot cocoa and eat cookies and let yourself be a kid again, Hope. Just this once."

She looked down at the costume and back up at him again. "You are *so* going to owe me for this."

And he was going to enjoy paying the price. "You'll do it?"

"I'll do it. For the kids, mind you."

"For the kids," he repeated. "You'd better get back to your cookies."

"The cookies! They've probably burned!" She rushed from the room, leaving the elf costume scattered on the bedspread and the scent of her perfume and dark chocolate behind.

He shook the bag of bells and smiled as the sound rang out. If this was the end of their time together he was at least going to give her a good memory to take away. He'd deal with his own feelings later.

Anna had saved the cookies from burning, and Hope had baked the rest without incident. They sat prettily on a plate now, dusted with icing sugar like snowy mountaintops. Hope had sneaked one earlier and they tasted as delicious as when Gram made them, making her long for the comforts of the one place she truly considered home.

Blake had remained scarce for most of the afternoon, getting the chores done ahead of his guests' arrival.

At three-thirty the kids and parents started arriving,

and the house became a hubbub of activity as Anna set out a Crock-Pot of hot cider, carafes of hot chocolate, plates of cookies and bowls of potato chips and pretzels.

Hope hadn't yet changed into her costume, and questioned whether or not she would. She would look ridiculous. Like an overgrown female Peter Pan with bells.

But when it came down to it she'd probably play along. She couldn't escape the memory of the look on Blake's face as he'd implored her to help him. Lordy, he was so handsome—and *kind*. She'd stopped noticing his scar days ago. What had once been ugly was now simply a part of the bigger whole, and that whole was something really special.

The carols playing on the stereo could barely be heard over the chatter and happy laughter of the kids. Cate arrived, using her crutches to get around, and Hope felt a surge of pleasure knowing that the little girl would have her sleigh ride complete with bells.

Hope looked around the busy room with a lump in her throat. This was how things should be, she realized. Loud and crazy and happy, with the sound of children's voices echoing through the house and the lingering scent of fresh-baked cookies in the air. It all felt so right that it caused an ache deep inside her. This was what she'd wanted for her sisters. For herself. And despite Gram's best efforts, and Hope's, it had never quite come to pass. But here—here it happened so effortlessly.

It was a bit of a miracle, really, and she wondered if Blake truly appreciated the magnitude of what he was doing with Bighorn. It was more than therapy. It was *home*. This was his family, she realized. Not by blood, but by love. He was the cord that bound them all together.

She blinked away a sheen of moisture on her eyes. If she wasn't careful she was going to leave a bit of herself behind when she left, and she wasn't sure she had too many pieces to spare.

"Ready for the first sleigh ride?" Blake's voice sounded close to her ear, the warmth of his breath sending tingles over her neck and down her spine.

"There's more than one?"

"I'll need to do two for sure, to fit everyone in."

"Won't I take up a valuable seat?" She turned her head slightly, angling her chin to look into his face.

His eyes were twinkling—he really enjoyed all this Christmas stuff, didn't he? He was going to make a wonderful Santa Claus. He'd make a wonderful father too—if he ever settled down and started a family. She wondered again why he hadn't.

"You can sit up with me," he said. "And get the carols started."

"Carols?"

He shook his head dolefully. "Hope, are you telling me you've never been on a sleigh ride?"

"Never."

"Then you'd best get your coat and boots and bundle up warm. It's high time you experienced one."

And then he was gone, to organize the first round of kids.

She met them outside, bundled as warm as she could be in heavy mittens and a hat, and one of Blake's goose-down jackets that was too big but the warmest thing she'd ever worn. The sleigh waited, hitched to two huge horses that stood so patiently Hope was sure they qualified as gentle giants. One shook his head, making the bells ring out merrily.

Cate clapped her hands at the sound. "Mister Blake, you *do* have bells!"

Blake tucked blankets around the knees of the passengers and rubbed the top of Cate's pom-pommed hat. "Didn't Hope promise you we would?"

Cate spun around to look at Hope. "You were right! He *does* have bells!"

The research, the drive, the money, the awkward moment with Blake this morning—all was worth it when she saw the smile on Cate's face.

"Of course!" she replied with a laugh. "What's a sleigh ride without bells?"

Hope climbed up front with Blake and nudged him with her elbow. "You've made Christmas for her, you know. Probably for all of them."

"They make mine, too," he replied quietly. He turned sideways and called back, "Everyone ready?"

"Yeah!" went up the chorus.

He gave the reins a gentle slap and the team started off. The runners squeaked on the snow, and Hope could smell the freshness of the air mingled with the pleasant smell of horses. Once they passed through the open gate to one of the pastures Blake urged the team into a trot, picking up the speed and causing some squeals in the back. Before long the first chorus of "Jingle Bells" started without any prompting from Hope, accompanied by the percussion of the bells on the harness. After "Jingle Bells" came "Silent Night," the young voices so sweet that Hope felt a stinging behind her eyes.

"You okay?"

She nodded. "You were right. This is special, Blake."

"Didn't you have fun Christmases at home?"

She shrugged. "Not so much. I tried, and Gram definitely tried, but most of the time either my parents were split and my dad was missing, or they were together and things were so tense that it just felt wrong, you know? After they split for good it was worse. We usually spent

Christmas with Gram, but our mother wasn't always around."

"I'm sorry, Hope."

She shrugged again, not wanting to delve too deeply into those feelings. "It is what it is, you know? I tried for a long time to step into that role, but it was a bit much to expect from a young girl. After a while I gave up."

"You were too young to be the mother."

She shrugged. "My sisters resented me for it, I think. I was only trying to help, but to them I was being bossy. I forgot how to have fun—thought that if I somehow kept things together maybe things would work out. That it would help Mom so she'd want to be around more. And if she were around more she'd be happier with Dad…" She paused, wondering how much to confess. "It was too much pressure to put on myself. The snowball fight the other day…? I haven't done anything spontaneous like that in years."

"Everything's precisely planned?"

"I don't get disappointed that way. I've had a lot of disappointments, Blake. I've learned not to have high expectations."

The song changed to the more upbeat "Rudolph the Red-Nosed Reindeer." The bells rang out merrily and the cold made their skin pink and vibrant.

"I hope you're not disappointed now," Blake replied, handling the reins easily in one gloved hand as they maneuvered through another gate into a grove of trees.

He put his free arm along the back of the seat, not quite an embrace, but she felt the intimacy of it anyway. It made her long to lean against his shoulder and let all her troubles go.

The tall spruces on either side made the setting even

better, adding the spicy scent of their needles to the winter potpourri.

"Today's a good day," she said simply, afraid to say any more lest emotion get the better of her.

Truthfully, today felt like a fairy tale. In her quest for perfection over the years she'd forgotten what it was like to enjoy simple pleasures. She'd pushed so much of her old life aside—things like hearing children's laughter and baking cookies and not worrying about how she looked and enjoying the moment.

Her quest for the perfect picture wasn't important right now. Perhaps it wasn't important at all anymore. She was living a sterile, scheduled existence, hiding behind a camera instead of participating in her own life.

She needed to fix that. She wasn't quite sure how, but she hoped that the trip to Beckett's Run would help. It was a start, anyway.

The horses picked up their pace as the back of the house came into view again, their necks bobbing as they led the way home.

"You coming on the next run?" Blake asked. "Or are you too cold?"

His shoulder buffered hers, and it would be so easy to slide over another inch or two and lean against him, swaying to the rhythm of the horses' gait. She was tempted, but she knew it wouldn't solve anything. Leaving was going to be difficult enough.

She shook her head. "I think I'll help Anna in the kitchen."

"Don't forget, when I get back it's Santa time."

Her heart thudded. "I haven't forgotten."

They pulled to a stop and Blake hopped down, then offered his hand to Hope to help her out of the seat. She put her mittened hand in his and jumped, landing so close to him the zippers of their jackets touched. For a prolonged second they paused, looking in each other's eyes.

Hope finally looked away. "Santa'd better get a move on," she murmured, and skirted around him toward the house.

As she went inside she heard his cheerful voice instructing the next round of kids where to sit, more laughter. She felt a strange sense of belonging and yet not belonging. Because this wasn't hers. She was only borrowing it for today. And it was getting harder and harder to remember that.

Blake had thought he was prepared for Hope as an elf, but he'd been very, very wrong.

Once the horses had been unhitched and put in their stalls he'd come in the back door to get ready for his stint as Santa. He was sneaking down the hall when he caught sight of her, all dressed in green. He should have known that, with her height, her legs would go on forever. The green tights clung to her legs, emphasizing the lean length of them, and the tunic with its scalloped edges skirted the tops of her thighs. Even with the ridiculous hat and shoes she was one heck of a sexy elf.

He changed into his Santa suit, stuffing the coat with a fat bed pillow and hooking the white beard over his ears before putting on his cap. Black boots rounded out the costume, and Anna had stitched him up a red sack made from fleece. Inside were presents for each child—a toy and a treat. He hadn't been extravagant, but that was hardly the point. Each item had been carefully chosen and wrapped.

"Ho, ho, ho!" he boomed, stepping into the living room with the sack over his shoulder.

Eyes widened, and one small voice whispered reverently, "It's Santa!"

Blake wasn't sure how convincing he was going to be—he was probably a good deal taller than most Santas, he only hoped the beard concealed his scar, and keeping up the deep, booming voice was going to be a challenge. But he took a seat in a chair by the tree and did his best.

"Santa's got a good little helper this year! Do you all know Hope? Doesn't she make a pretty elf?"

He nearly laughed at the mortified expression on Hope's face as all eyes turned to her.

"Well," she replied, clearing her throat, "if Santa came *all* this way for our party, it's only right he should have a helping hand, don't you think?"

"Yeah!"

Excitement bubbled up and out, and everyone looked to Blake again. Hope sent him a wink that said she knew what he was up to—and she was going along with it.

"Hope, maybe you can give Santa a hand by taking the presents out of that sack." He looked down at the children. "Did you all want presents? My elves have worked very hard this year. I hope you've all been good."

"I've been good, Thanta!" one girl called out with an adorable lisp.

There were more shouts and laughs and Blake chuckled at one little boy who was so excited he was almost vibrating.

Dutifully Hope came forward and reached into the bag, pulling out the first present. She handed it to him and he let his eyes twinkle up at her. Little did she know, but this was only the first of the surprises in store for her today.

"Says here this present is for Chad," Blake boomed. "Come on up, Chad, and get your present."

Chad, who had suffered a spinal cord injury when he was three, shuffled up to Blake with a wide smile. "For me?"

"For you," Blake said, handing over the present.

And so it went on until, just as he'd planned, there was one box left in the bottom of the sack.

"Ho, ho, ho," he said deeply as he picked it up. "It feels like there is something else in here."

Hope had a wrinkle between her eyebrows. "But everyone has a present," she said.

He reached into the bag and took out the small box. "Says here this one is for Hope. Ho, ho, ho!" He looked up at her expectantly. "Hope, come sit on Santa's knee while he gives you your present." He patted his thigh.

"I think I'll stand—thanks anyway, Santa."

"Sit on his knee!" called Cate.

"Yeah," shouted a few others, "sit on Santa's lap, Hope!"

With a dark look aimed just at him, Hope came closer and perched on his knee. "I'll get you for this," she murmured, just loud enough that he could hear.

"I'm counting on it," he whispered back, but then continued on in his booming, jolly voice, "Now, Santa has a long trip after this, so I think he needs a little something to keep him warm."

"Hot chocolate!" shouted someone.

His grin widened. "Need to watch the waistline," he said, patting his round stomach. "After all, I'll be getting lots of milk and cookies very soon. What about a kiss from Hope here?" He touched a finger to his cheek. "Come on, Hope. Give Santa a kiss."

Her eyes were like daggers, but she smiled sweetly and dutifully pecked his cheek. "Santa's beard is scratchy," she announced.

He handed over the present. "Don't open it here," he whispered, then boosted her off his lap and picked up the empty bag. "Well, Santa must be getting back. Reindeer-training, you know. Merry Christmas, everyone!"

He added in a few extra *ho, ho, ho*s as he waded

through wads of wrapping paper to the door and slipped outside. Then he made his way to the back of the house and stripped down to his T-shirt and long johns. So no curious eyes would catch sight of the bright red suit he left the suit on the back step to collect later and hurried out of the cold, darting inside and sneaking to his room, where he changed into his jeans and shirt. He pulled on his jacket, went out the back door and around to the front, and made a show of coming back in again.

"What'd I miss?"

"Oh, Mister Blake, Santa was here!" Cate's excitement quivered in her voice. "And he got me a new doll!"

"Santa? When I was stuck out in the barn putting the horses up for the night?"

"You missed it! Hope sat on his knee and kissed him an' everything!"

His gaze strayed to Hope. She was still in her elf getup, still strikingly beautiful. As their eyes met he suddenly wished for the party to be over, so he could put the next part of his plan in motion.

This was their last night together. No more television in the evenings. No more watching her work on her laptop with those silly glasses on her face. No more kisses in the snow or by the flickering light of the tree. He didn't want the day to be over, but he did want the evening to get started. He'd promised her a good memory, after all. He wanted it, too. If this was all he was going to have from her he wanted it to be a night to remember.

"Well, I'm sorry I missed *that*," he replied to Cate, dragging his eyes away from Hope.

"Okay, everyone, before you go I want a group picture," Hope called out, picking up her camera once more. "In front of the tree. Blake, you get on your knees. And, moms and dads, if you could help out…"

Blake followed orders, wondering how Hope was dealing with the chaos of trying to set the shot. She was always so worried about lighting and balance and things being in the right place. But before he knew it she was directing them to smile and say "Merry Christmas" and it was over.

Things started to wind down after that; parents got kids ready to go home, Anna and Hope began clearing away platters and bowls and cups.

Blake retrieved his Santa suit and put it away, and as Hope changed out of her elf costume he packed a Thermos of fresh cocoa and a basket of goodies. It was fully dark outside, crisp and cool, and if his hunch was right nature was going to put on a show later tonight. A show he didn't want Hope to miss.

CHAPTER TEN

HOPE packed away the elf costume and changed back into her jeans and a fuzzy sweater with pockets. She tucked Blake's present inside one, running her fingers over the foil wrapping and soft ribbon. Her lips still tingled from kissing his cheek, and the fake beard had been soft, not scratchy as she'd said.

The whole day had been disturbingly perfect—a word she didn't use often. But there wasn't another word to describe the way she was feeling. Happy. Complete. Wonderful.

Perfect.

The only thing marring the perfection was knowing it was going to be over and tomorrow she'd be saying goodbye.

Anna was putting on her coat when Hope wandered back to the kitchen.

"I'll see you in the morning, yeah?" Anna asked. "To see you off?"

"I don't leave until eleven," Hope assured her, a heavy feeling settling in her stomach.

She really was leaving here tomorrow. On the one hand she was actually looking forward to seeing Gram and her sisters…and, if she were being honest, even her mom and dad, if what Faith said about them getting along was true.

But on the other hand, she was going to be sad to leave. Only a little over a week ago she'd been determined to find a hotel and stay somewhere else. Now it was hard to imagine spending Christmas anywhere else.

As Anna's car pulled out of the drive Blake came back in. It felt odd somehow, intimate, and with a layer of tension that was unexpected just by being alone together. He had his outdoor gear on again, and she wondered if he had late-night chores that needed doing.

"Bundle up," he suggested, standing in the doorway. "Night's not over yet."

A strange sort of twirling started through her tummy as his gaze seemed to bore straight through to the heart of her. "It's not?"

"Not by a long shot. I have something to show you. I hope. Meet me outside in five minutes?"

She nodded. It was their last night. She couldn't imagine not going along with whatever he had planned.

When Hope stepped outside first she heard the bells. Once down the steps and past the snowbank she saw that Blake had hitched the horses to the sleigh again. It was dark, but the sliver of moon cast an ethereal glow on the snow and the stars twinkled in the inky sky. A moonlight sleigh ride. She'd guessed there was something of the romantic in him, but this went beyond her imagining.

The practical side of her cautioned her to be careful. But the other side…the side that craved warmth and romance and intimacy…the side that she'd packaged carefully away years ago so as to protect it…urged her to get inside the sleigh and take advantage of every last bit of holiday romance she could. It was fleeting, after all. And too good to miss.

Blake sat on the bench in the driver's seat, reins in his left hand while he held out his right. "Come with me?"

She gripped his hand and stepped up and onto the seat. He'd placed a blanket on the wood this time, a cushion against the hard surface. A basket sat in between their feet.

Blake smiled. "Ready?"

Ready for what? She knew he meant the ride, but right now the word seemed to ask so much more. She nodded, half exhilarated, half terrified, as he drove them out of the barnyard and on a different route—back to the pasture where they'd first taken the snowmobile. The bells called out in rhythm with the hoofbeats, the sound keeping them company in the quiet night.

Neither said anything until they reached the ridge several minutes later. The foothills rolled in shadow, a palette of grays and blacks that curled up next to the mountains. Blake hooked the reins and reached down for the basket.

"We didn't have a proper dinner, but if you can stand a few more cookies I can." He opened a container with an assortment of sweets, and then took out two mugs and a Thermos. "And hot chocolate with a little extra something."

He poured her a cup and handed it over, steam curling into the air with the rich scent of creamy chocolate. She took the cup in both hands, leaving her mitts on. At the first sip she grinned—he'd laced it with Irish Cream.

"Delicious," she said, peeling off a mitten and reaching for a cookie. "And proper dinner is overrated anyway."

The heat of the chocolate and the buttery richness of the cookies soon had her feeling warm and lazy, and she leaned back against Blake's shoulder, looking up at the sky.

"The sky is so big here," she whispered, staring at the carpet of stars. "Do you know that in Australia I don't see the Big Dipper?" She angled her head so she was looking at his profile. "It's like we don't even see the same sky, Blake."

The thought made her feel disconnected and lonely. It would have been nice to go home and at least think that maybe they were looking at the same thing, even though they were miles apart. But it was a foolish, romantic notion. The time difference didn't even add up. It was the kind of thing Hope the romantic would have thought of when she was fifteen. Not the realistic Hope at thirty.

They sat in silence for a long time, gazing at the stars, sipping their chocolate, until Blake pointed toward the north horizon. "Well, you won't see this in Australia," he said, his voice holding a note of excitement. "Hope—look."

She followed his finger and stared at the sky. "What am I looking at?"

"Give it another second…*there*. See it?"

The sky somehow shifted before her eyes. There was a swirling and a wash of white, like spilled milk, that suddenly caught edges of green and hints of yellow.

She sat up straight in the sleigh and stared. "Oh, wow! That's the northern lights, isn't it?"

"I hoped—with the moon not so full tonight and it being so clear and cold. You can't always see them this far south. Up north, around Fort McMurray, they're amazing. Bigger, more colors."

"Oh, but this is amazing, too, Blake. Look at that."

It was like the ripples of a blanket, all curves and shifts and soft hues. She was suddenly overwhelmed by it all—the sleigh, the picnic, the stars. It was like Blake was bewitched, able to take all the elements of a perfect winter night and hold them in the palm of his hand, releasing each one like a wish at his command. Even the Aurora Borealis. How did she stand a chance against such a man?

"I wish you didn't have to go tomorrow," he said, his voice low in his chest. "I wish you could stay for Christmas. Meet my parents. Have eggnog in your coffee Christmas morning and eat bacon and waffles and unwrap presents in your pajamas."

"It sounds lovely," she said wistfully, reluctantly drawing her gaze away from nature's display. "But I promised Gram. And I need to see my family. I didn't realize how much until I came here."

"So your grandmother's plan *did* work?" he commented, sipping his chocolate, which she now figured had to be cold because they'd stargazed so long.

"Gram's always known me better than everyone else. When I told you today that I gave up trying…I'd been burning the candle at both ends and I blew my exams. I lost a big scholarship and at eighteen—well, it felt like my life was over. Gram was there for that. She was the one who stepped in and made it right. It was the lowest I ever remember being until…"

"Until Julie died?"

"Yes." She breathed out the word with relief. "Julie was the first person I'd trusted in a long time. We were like sisters only without all the drama." She gave a small smile. "Losing her was…"

They watched the lights a little longer, until Blake interrupted the silence, carrying on with her last thought as if there'd never been a break in the conversation.

"Only you didn't really grieve. Which is why you reacted the way you did when you saw me."

"You know it is." She finished the last mouthful of lukewarm chocolate and tucked her mug back into the basket. "But, Blake, I stopped thinking about your scar after the first few days. It's not all there is to you. I know that. You're so much more. You're…" She stopped before she could say *everything.*

"Maybe you're more than your scars, too, Hope. Have you considered that?"

She swallowed thickly. "Of course I've considered it."

"But you're afraid?"

"Wouldn't you be?"

They sat in silence for a few more moments.

"I think I need to start doing that, Blake. Grieving for Julie, I mean. She came from a messed-up family, too. She respected that there was stuff I just didn't talk about. She didn't expect anything of me, which was a revelation. I let myself rely on her, and then she was gone."

Really gone. No second chances, forever gone.

The stars blurred and the lights disappeared as she blinked rapidly. "After the funeral I had to go home and pack up her things. I had to meet with her mother and send everything back. I had to go home to an empty apartment every night. I missed her." She swiped her hand over her face. "I do miss her. And I'm angry."

Blake put his arm around her and held her close against his side. "Angry with her for leaving?"

"Of course! That's what people *do,* Blake. They teach you to love them and count on them and then they leave. It's not worth it."

"Of course it is. It just hurts. It hurts when I think of Brad, but I can't imagine not having those years with him, not having those memories. Not everyone leaves, Hope. You've just had more than your share."

"The last week or so has been good for me," she admitted. "But it's a small bit of time. Temporary. It's not really my life. I needed it, yes. But now I have to figure out what comes next. Some of that is reconnecting with my family."

"And after that?"

"I don't know."

She really didn't. She had her job and her apartment in Sydney, but the thought of it seemed empty and lonely now. There would be no Gram. No Blake. No one who really mattered.

He took her mittened hands in his. "Come back."

"What?" Her gaze darted to his and she found his eyes dark and utterly earnest.

"Come back. I don't have all the answers, but I don't want tomorrow to be goodbye forever. There's something between us, Hope. I know you've felt it, too."

"Well, of course I felt it. But like I said, it's temporary."

"Why should it have to be?" He turned in the seat and gripped her wrists. "I've seen you with the kids, I've seen the way you light up. I know you've had a hard time of it and you're cautious. Don't you think I understand? This quest for perfection…it's what you rely on. You don't want to be disappointed. I get it. And I also know how I feel when you're around, Hope. I light up. I haven't felt this way in a really long time."

"It's just Christmas. People get all weird and sentimental at the holidays," she answered, but her voice felt tight and choked in her throat.

The worst of it was she suspected he really did get it. And she wanted to believe him. Wanted it so badly because it meant she wouldn't be alone.

"It's not just Christmas," he contradicted.

He leaned forward and pressed his forehead to hers, the thick knit of their caps touching. He kissed the tip of her nose before dipping lower and kissing her lips gently, sweetly, so perfectly that she half expected Christmas angels to start singing right above the northern lights. She allowed herself a taste of him…chocolate and the nip of whiskey cream, and butter and a man. A delicious com-

bination that was tough to resist. The problem was tha
Blake was perfect. And for the first time in her life sh
didn't trust perfection.

"Be reasonable," she said, pulling away from the kiss
running her tongue over her lips for one last tantalizing
taste. "We've only known each other ten days, Blake."

"I know, and that's why I want you to come back. S
we can figure this out."

She shook her head, feeling the beginnings of pani
settling in, cramping her chest, making it hard to breath
in the frigid air. "My job is in Sydney. My apartment i
there. My life is there. I can't just pick up and leave whe
I want. I have obligations."

"Another few weeks," he suggested. "You never vaca
tion. You must have time coming to you."

"And then what?" she asked, sliding away, putting
inches between them.

He was going to make her say it, make it difficul
wasn't he?

"I leave after a few more weeks and it's even harde
to say goodbye? It wouldn't work, Blake. You've buil
something amazing here. The program is your life an
it's important. You can't just pick up and leave eithe
You belong here. And I'm not crazy enough to pack u
and leave my life behind after ten days of…whatever it'
been, with no guarantees."

"And you need guarantees?" he said coldly.

"You know I do. Come on, Blake. What happens to m
if suddenly it doesn't work out? How can I give up th
little security I've built? And what would I do? No hom
no job…" She lowered her voice, leaving out the most im
portant word…*alone*. "I'm not resilient enough for that.

"Then…" He lifted his chin. "People do the long-dis
tance thing every day."

Her heart sank. This was not how she'd wanted things to go. She'd wanted to leave smiling and with fond memories, not with hurt feelings and...well, broken dreams seemed a little dramatic, but it was certainly feeling that way at this moment.

"Be realistic, Blake. Canada to Australia? Long distance aside, how often would we see each other? Do you know the cost of flights between Calgary and Sydney?"

"You're not even willing to try," he accused, sitting back against the seat of the sleigh. "You're going to leave tomorrow and write me off, the way you write off everyone who disappoints you!"

"That's not true," she defended. "I don't write people off. They write *me* off." She was getting angry now, was tired of always being made to feel like she was the one lacking. "I didn't kill Julie, and I sure as hell didn't ask my parents to split up and drag us from pillar to post so that we never really knew what home was. I'm the one who tried to keep the family together, and instead we ended up scattered all over the damn globe. That's not my fault!"

"I know," he said quietly. "And now you know it, too."

Silence settled uncomfortably as Hope sat there, feeling worn-out and, worse, played.

"I told you in the beginning that I didn't need to be fixed." Her voice was low and held a distinct warning. "I'm not one of your clients, Blake. I didn't come here to be psychoanalyzed. You said you were a rancher with an ear, but that's not true. You're a fixer."

"That's unfair—" he started, but Hope held up a hand.

"You fix people. That's what you do. You need to be needed. You see someone hurt and you make them better. You find someone troubled and you give them the answers—the kids that come here and even Anna."

"Anna?"

"She needed money and you gave her a job. She told me things about herself—about how she lost her husband when she was so young and brought up John on her own. And Blake swooped in to the rescue, right?"

"When did helping people become a flaw?" he defended.

"Why do you suppose you try to fix everyone? Does it have anything to do with not being able to save your brother?"

He couldn't have looked more shocked if she'd slapped him and she instantly felt sorry for the words. Losing his brother had been devastating; she knew that.

She sighed. "I'm sorry. That was uncalled for."

"No, you're right. I couldn't save Brad. But I can help others rather than letting the accident and my loss cripple me."

She understood the implication, even agreed with it. In his grief he'd found a way to reach out. *She'd* found a way to withdraw and protect herself.

She swallowed against the lump in her throat. "Oh, Blake. What happens when I'm all fixed? Will you be done with me then? Or what happens when you figure out that you can't fix me? Do you give up and walk away?"

"It wouldn't be like that."

But he couldn't know that, and they both knew it.

"Why haven't you ever married, Blake? It's clear you'd make a great father, so what's holding you back?"

He looked nonplussed, sitting back against the seat of the sleigh and staring at her with wide eyes. "What do you mean? I suppose I haven't found the right person."

"And will you ever? Face it, Blake. You're married to the program and those kids are your children. You get to fix them and send them on their way. Yes, you get close to them—but not too close, right? Because then you don't have to be afraid of losing them the way you lost your brother."

He looked so shocked she knew she'd gotten it right. She lowered her voice. "You made them your family so you don't have to take a risk on your own, didn't you? So how can you ask me to take a risk on you if you're not capable of doing the same?"

"Hope…" he said hoarsely. But that was all.

He had no rebutting argument. Hope felt relieved that the truth was out, but horrible that she hadn't been kinder with it. Blake deserved better.

If they'd been back at the house she would have made her apologies and left it at that. She would have walked away before they could hurt each other further. But where could she go here? She was stuck in his sleigh in the middle of nowhere. What would she do? Walk home? In the dark?

She pulled away and stared stubbornly at her boots. "I think we should go back now."

"So you can run away again?"

"Maybe I'm running *to* something this time."

He sighed and studied his hands. "I'm not saying you're wrong," he admitted. "Hope, despite everything we've said to each other, everything that's happened, you must know I care about you."

He looked up and met her gaze, so earnest and artless her heart turned over a little bit.

"I know you're hurting. Tonight when I looked at you I could tell that you wanted to belong so very badly. You do, Hope. More than you know. You *do* belong."

They'd argued and struck nerves and he still managed to see past it. The truth was he could never know how badly she wanted to stay. To see where things might go between them. And perhaps if she didn't live half a world away she would try it.

But her job was there—a good job—and it would be foolish to throw her career away for a maybe. Her mother chased those sorts of rainbows. Hope didn't. She knew how awful the thud could be at the end. She wasn't sure she could bounce back one more time.

"I can't," she said, her voice raw. "I'm sorry, Blake."

He looked at her for one long moment before picking up the reins and giving the team a slap. The sleigh lurched forward and Hope hugged her arms around herself. The wind picked up and the cold seeped through her coat and mittens.

It seemed to take forever to get back to the house. Blake halted the horses and Hope jumped out, grabbing the basket and taking it with her.

"I've got to look after the team," Blake said.

"Good night," she answered. "Thank you for the ride."

It was paltry and it rang a little false. The first part had been magical and then it had all fallen apart.

"I'll see you in the morning," he replied, and with a *hup* he had the sleigh moving again toward the barn.

Morning. As Hope turned toward the house she felt the first cold tear slip down her cheek. On one hand her leaving seemed too soon, but on the other she wanted it over with. Maybe then she could stop hurting. Because what Blake didn't understand was how badly she'd wanted to say yes. How much she'd wanted to be able to trust blindly and take a leap.

She was falling in love with him—perhaps had been from the start. And he'd offered her no guarantees because there were none.

She wouldn't have believed him even if he had, because deep down they both knew guarantees didn't exist.

CHAPTER ELEVEN

BLAKE made sure the chores were done and he was inside by midmorning. Hope was planning on leaving by eleven, and already a light snow was falling. The roads probably weren't going to be bad, but there was no guarantee of that.

Guarantee. There was that word again. She was expecting the impossible. He'd stopped believing in absolutes when Brad had died in that crash. He'd offered her more time—their time together had been too short; he was just now starting to really understand what he felt for her. It didn't really have anything to do with fixing her, did it?

And yet her words still echoed in his head, because he thought she might be right. He'd invested in his surrogate family because the idea of going through what he'd gone through—what his parents had gone through—after Brad died wasn't anything he wanted to experience again. Whether it had been intentional or not, that was what he'd done. And it had been easier to let Cindy go and say it was about her nonacceptance of his scar than it was to face the fact that he'd done exactly what Hope had done—protected his heart from being hurt again.

He was wiping dishes for Anna when Hope came downstairs, carrying her suitcase. She was dressed in her silly boots again and the wool jacket that looked like a winter coat but which they both knew was useless against real cold. Her hair was up in some sort of artistic twist and her makeup was flawless.

Oh, yes, her barriers were well in place, weren't they? And he'd been the one to make them go back up after he'd worked so hard to tear them down.

"You're all ready," Anna observed, drying her hands on Blake's dish towel.

"Ready as I'll ever be," Hope replied, trying to sound perky.

But he heard the wobble.

"I have something for you," Anna said, going to her recipe book. "Recipes for your favorites." She held out a sheaf of cards. "It's not much, but…"

Blake watched as Hope took them.

"It's perfect," she said warmly. "Whenever I get to missing this place I'll be able to make them and think of you. Thanks, Anna, for making me feel so welcome while I was here."

"You take care."

Anna barely came up to Hope's chin but Hope bent down a little and gave Anna a hug.

"You, too," she replied.

Anna stood back and flapped the dish towel at Blake. "Go on," she said. "Get out of my kitchen, you two, so I can get some work done."

He knew what she was doing. Making sure he and Hope had a smidgen of privacy to say goodbye. But voices carried in the house.

Blake followed Hope down the hall to the front door. "Wait a sec. I'll put on my boots and help you with your bag."

Hope paused by the door. "I left a CD with my pictures on it on top of your desk," she said quietly. "My email's there, too, if you have any questions or need a little more editing. I've saved them all."

So a glimmer of hope for more contact. But not nearly enough, and more of a formality than an invitation.

"Thank you." He opened the door and picked up her suitcase. "Careful. We've had a bit of snow. The walk could be slippery."

Like it had been when she'd arrived. He remembered seeing her go down, flat on her back, and the moment his breath had caught, hoping she hadn't hurt herself. That same breathlessness had happened again when she'd taken his hand and he'd helped her to her feet.

And again the first time he'd kissed her when they'd decorated the tree.

Damn. That had been the moment. The precise second that he'd begun his freefall, when he'd dropped the shield around his heart and let her in in a way he'd never let anyone in before.

She popped the trunk of her rental and he stowed the bag inside. "Be careful. The highway should be fine, but these side roads might be slippery. Is your phone charged?"

"Of course. Don't worry. I've got time. My flight doesn't leave for a few hours."

She stopped by the driver's-side door and fiddled with the keys. She was as nervous as he was, it seemed. It hadn't been this awkward since the very beginning between them.

"Hope, about last night..."

"I'm sorry," she whispered, looking up at him with tortured eyes. "I shouldn't have said what I did. I didn't mean to hurt you."

"Nor I you." He stopped just short of admitting she was right; it wouldn't change a darned thing now. She was determined to go and nothing would change her mind. Not even if he bared his heart and soul to her. "I don't want you leaving with this negativity between us. I want a good memory to hold on to when you're gone."

She swallowed, her throat bobbing as her lower lip quivered.

"Ah, hell," he said, giving up and stepping in.

He cupped his hand around her neck, feeling the soft skin beneath his fingers and the silky texture of her hair. If this was the last time he was going to see her, he'd be damned sure to kiss her goodbye.

Her mouth opened beneath his and she gave a little breathy sigh that only served to fuel both his desire and his frustration. Maybe she was right. Maybe it was impossible. At the very least it was crazy to feel this way after such a short time. He nibbled on her lower lip for just a moment before pulling away. And yet he still held her, one hand on the nape of her neck and the other resting on her rib cage, unwilling to let her go, because when he did it would be for good.

He was relatively certain now that the feelings he had went deeper than he had ever expected. Why else would it hurt so much to watch her leave? He kept the words inside, though, not wanting to make it any harder for either of them to say goodbye. Because they must say it. There was no other thing to do.

"I've got to get going," she whispered.

"I know."

He reached around her and opened her door. "Be safe."

She got in behind the wheel and started the car, letting the engine warm up. A swipe of the windshield wipers swept the snow away from the glass.

Blake kept his hand on the top of the door for one more

minute. "Merry Christmas, Hope. Enjoy your time with your family."

"Merry Christmas, Blake."

He shut her door, not wanting to, not knowing what else to do.

She started off down the lane and he watched as she reached the road and turned left, heading out toward the highway, on to Calgary, to Massachusetts, to Australia.

A world away.

It was only when she was out of sight that he remembered she hadn't opened his present.

Beckett's Run hadn't changed much. Even at night it was clear the old businesses were much the same. And, like it did every year, the town had gone all out in Christmas decorating—perhaps even more than Hope remembered. Lights twinkled like multicolored stars, porches were strung with evergreen garlands, and the statue of town founder Andrew Beckett sported a plush wreath around his neck. Even nature had been accommodating, supplying a blanket of pure white snow for the holiday.

A few weeks ago Hope would have rolled her eyes at the blatant demonstration of peace and goodwill toward men. But now the familiarity of being home made the backs of her eyes sting as she drove through town in yet another rented car, heading toward her grandmother's house. She'd found them stinging more often than she was comfortable with ever since leaving Alberta.

Despite her resolve, she'd left a bit of herself behind, after all.

She turned the corner and saw Gram's house. A delighted laugh escaped her lips. The blue Cape Cod–style house was decorated just like it had been when they'd been kids—every single shrub and tree frosted with lights, a giant wreath on the door, and a candy cane walkway lead-ing to the porch. She pulled in the yard and cut the engine, content just to look at it for a while, feeling the fulfillment of being *home*. She should have come back before now. Should have made the time instead of avoiding the place.

She got out of the car, and had grabbed her suitcase from the back when the front door opened and Gram stood in the doorway, wearing a reindeer apron and a wide smile.

"You're here!" she called, excitement and welcome fill-ing her voice.

"I'm here," Hope answered, grinning, and then on im-pulse she left her suitcase in the snow and ran up the steps to give her grandmother a hug.

"Oh, my precious girl," Gram said, hugging her back. "I wasn't sure you'd come."

"Of course I came."

"And the drive?"

"The drive was lovely. Roads were terrific."

Gram stood back and held her by the arms. "Have you eaten?"

Hope shook her head. It was the same old pattern and it felt good: love, questions, followed by food. "I only had a sandwich on the plane."

"Hours ago," Gram stated. "Bring in your bag and I'll heat up some chowder."

Hope took her bag inside and slid off her boots before carting it up to her old bedroom. The spread and wall-paper were exactly the same as they'd been the last time she'd visited—just before taking the Sydney job. In the desk drawer were old notebooks and pens, and a really old lip gloss that had dried out but had once been waxy and strawberry-flavored.

Gram had kept all her things just as she'd left them. In the hope that one day Hope would come home? An ache spread across her chest. For all her grievances and reasons she knew they were mere excuses. She had stayed away too long. Gram deserved better. If anything had come from this trip at all it was her determination that she'd get it.

Back downstairs, Hope got a good look at her grandmother. A little older, but still with her cheerful face, sparkling eyes, and soft white hair. She wore a sweater with a holly pattern on it. Gram had always loved the holidays, no matter what was going on. Maybe she was getting older, but she kept herself young.

"Sit down, honey. I've got some fresh bread to go with that."

Hope sat at the table and looked around. "Oh, it's good to be home," she said at last, as Mary put a bowl in front of her. "Where's Grace?"

"Oh, I'm guessing she's with J.C., putting the final touches on the plans for the festival tomorrow. She's been helping him out, you know."

"Grace? And J.C.? Working together?" She raised an eyebrow and gave her grandmother a telling look. "How many trips to the E.R.?"

Gram's face took on an innocent expression. "They seem to be getting along just fine."

"And Faith?"

"Faith and Marcus arrive tomorrow."

"Faith *and Marcus?*"

Hope's spoon clattered to the bowl. *What?* Last she'd spoken to Faith she'd claimed the Earl was getting on her nerves. But then, Hope remembered, there *had* been a particular tone in her voice that suggested something quite different…

"It appears Faith has decided to hold on to her earl," Gram said, picking at the crust of a slice of bread. She put it down, folded her hands on the table and looked at Hope. "And what about you, dear? How was your trip to Alberta?"

Hope studied her bowl. "It was good. Mr. Nelson..." how strange it was to call him that! "...has a great facility, and the children were wonderful. I left him with a CD full of pictures."

"And that's it?" Gram sounded disappointed.

Hope schooled her features and looked up. "Was there supposed to be more?" she asked innocently.

Gram watched her closely but didn't say anything.

"You wouldn't have been playing matchmaker, would you, Gram?" She sent her grandmother a sly look.

"Of course not!" Gram protested, but roses appeared on her cheeks. "Well, maybe. He's very good-looking, and right around your age, and I know he's from good people..."

Hope fought the urge to laugh and patted Gram's hand. "This chowder is as good as I remember. And the ten days away were good for me—so you're forgiven for issuing ultimatums."

Mary's face relaxed. "It's good to see you, Hope. I never thought I'd see all my girls under one roof again."

"It's good to be back."

But a bit of Hope was still stuck in a sleigh in an arctic breeze, watching the northern lights. She missed it already—the coziness of the log house, the barn, the sight of the mountains in the distance and Anna's cooking in the kitchen while Blake teased.

How was it she could be homesick for a place she hardly knew? She'd only been there for a few days. And she'd been gone for hours, not years.

"You all right, Hope?"

Hope shook the thoughts away. "Just tired. I think I might have a hot bath and an early night. Can we catch up more tomorrow?"

"Of course we can. You go ahead. I'm not going to be far behind you. Gotta keep up my energy for tomorrow's hoopla."

Hope kissed her grandmother good night and headed up the stairs. In the bathroom the scent of pink rose soap was in the air—a scent she always associated with Gram. She started the bath and went to her room while it was running to open her suitcase and take out pajamas. She found the flannel pants toward the bottom and was pulling them out when Blake's present fell out onto the floor.

She picked it up and examined the wrapping, touching it with her fingertips, feeling the texture of the silver foil and the soft curve of the ribbon. She went to the bathroom and turned off the bath, and then went back and sat on her bed. Slowly she untied the ribbon, putting it carefully on her dresser. She split the tape with a fingernail, wanting for some odd reason to leave the paper perfectly intact.

Inside was a square box. She removed the lid to find an exquisite dream catcher inside, lying on a nest of soft cotton.

She lifted it out, admiring the intricate weave and the gorgeous gray and black feathers drifting down. She wondered if Anna had made it. She wouldn't be surprised; the woman could do just about anything.

Folded on top of the cotton was a note. Her heart pounded as she took it out of the box and opened it.

There are different stories of the dream catcher, but this is my favorite: the hole in the center of the dream catcher is to let good dreams pass through

*and bless your sleep. The web is to catch all your
bad dreams so they disappear with the dawn.*
   May all your dreams be sweet ones, Hope.
   All my love, Blake

All my love. Hope stared at the note, stared again at the
beads and feathers, and touched each bit tenderly.

All my love. The words repeated in her head and she bit
down on her lip. Was that the feeling she couldn't seem to
pinpoint? Was it love? It must be, because why else would
she feel so miserable?

CHAPTER TWELVE

CHRISTMAS Eve morning dawned as all Christmas Eve mornings should—cold, clear, with a robin's-egg-blue sky and beams of sunlight that bounced off crystalline snow.

Hope slept in past the sunrise, waking shortly after nine. In Alberta it would be just past seven. Blake was probably up already and finished with the chores. His parents would arrive today from Phoenix for the holiday. He'd open his presents tomorrow, including the one she'd placed under the tree for him before she left.

The idea made her so lonely she curled up in the covers once more, soaking in the last bit of warmth.

But it was Christmas Eve, and there were things to be done. The festival was today, and events were going on all over town. She forced herself out of bed, straightened the covers, and looked in the mirror.

Should she straighten her hair? She looked at the curls tumbling over her shoulders, tighter than usual because it had still been damp when she went to bed. She'd been straightening it for years, but today she wanted to let it go. It looked...relaxed. And she was going to try to relax more. Accept things as they were rather than trying to be in control.

Besides, everyone in Beckett's Run would remember her with corkscrew curls. She smiled to herself as she dressed in jeans and a long-sleeved T-shirt. Why shouldn't she enjoy the holiday? There'd be street vendors with food and hot chocolate, music and events all over town.

And if she joined in maybe she wouldn't think of Blake quite so much.

That plan was soundly thwarted when she arrived downstairs. Grace was standing at the kitchen counter, pouring a cup of coffee. When Hope walked in Grace simply got another cup out of the cupboard and poured her a drink.

"Hey," Hope said quietly, wondering if Grace was still mad at her. Their last conversation hadn't exactly gone well. "Where's Gram?"

"Hey, yourself." Grace handed over the cup. "Gram's helping out with one of the events today. She said you went to bed early. I got in late…"

"I heard you. That board on the porch, remember?" Hope grinned at her sister. "It always did cause you trouble. With J.C. then, too, if I remember right."

Grace raised an eyebrow. "There was a lot to do to get ready for today. I need to be out the door soon." She paused. "It's good to see you, Hope."

"Really?" Hope sat down at the table. "After our last talk…"

But Grace waved a hand. "It doesn't matter now. It was good for me to come back. To see Gram. To…"

But she didn't finish the sentence. "Anyway, how was ranch life? Gram said you were taking pictures for some therapy-type place."

"It was good." Hope felt her cheeks heat but ignored it. "It's a therapeutic riding facility. I took pictures, had a chance to recharge."

"Is that all?"

The same question Gram had asked. Suddenly Hope

felt like she needed her sister very much. Perhaps that had been a lot of the problem—she'd never let herself confide in Grace or Faith. She hadn't wanted to burden them with her troubles. But they were all grown up now. And, while Hope didn't want to spill her guts to Gram and get her hopes up, she had the strange urge to tell Grace everything.

"No, it's not all." Shyness and a fear of being rejected made her backpedal. "But I doubt you want to hear it."

Grace sat down at the table. "Try me."

"I thought you had to skedaddle?"

"I can manage a few minutes."

Something passed between them then—a simple sort of acceptance, a closeness that had been missing for too long. "The guy that owns the place—Blake—and I…we kind of got involved."

"How involved?"

Hope felt her face flame yet again. "There's a slim chance I may have fallen a little bit in love with him."

Grace sat back in her chair and laughed. "A *slim* chance? You *may* have…? Oh, Hope. You haven't really changed, have you?"

"What do you mean?"

"You always hold back, refuse to let in people who would help you. Who would care for you. You're so busy protecting yourself from getting hurt that you forget how to live in the process."

"Don't sugarcoat it on my account," Hope said, still feeling the sting of Grace's words. "I'm sorry I said anything."

She made a move to get up, but Grace's next words made her sit right back down again.

"Does he love you, too?"

Did he? He hadn't said as much.

"I don't know. He asked if I'd come back after Christmas for a while. But it's impossible, right? I mean… I live in Australia. It's no way to run a relationship. And I'm hardly going to throw all that away after a ten-day… well, whatever. Flirtation?"

"You want to know how I see it?" Grace pushed her coffee cup across the table. "You were the oldest. You tried really hard to fill the gaps, especially when we weren't here with Gram. You tried to be perfect for everyone. But no one is perfect, Hope. And no matter what any of us did you were the responsible one. Faith never wanted to rock the boat, and me…? Well, I tried to get attention in other ways. But none of it made a bit of difference. And now you're so afraid of getting hurt that you push everyone away."

She reached over and in a move that was so not Grace, touched Hope's hand.

"I know a lot of people think I'm the most like Mom. I never stay in one place for long. I'm always after the next thing. But I think *you* are, Hope. Because you are spending so much time fighting who you really are by trying to be who you think you ought to be. No wonder you're exhausted."

In an odd, twisted way Grace made perfect sense.

"I'm scared," Hope admitted. There was a slight tremor in her voice; it was a tough thing to confess. "I'm scared to take that leap."

"After our upbringing, of course you are! All I'm saying is don't let your job stop you. If you love him, wouldn't he be worth it? You're a brilliant photographer, Hope. Why else did you think I asked you to do that assignment with me? I've been freelancing for years—nothing to say you can't do the same. Your job is just an excuse."

Hope chuckled. "Today is one day I appreciate your

bluntness," she said. "I'll think about it. In the meantime, there's Christmas to get through, right?"

She didn't have to decide anything right now.

"Which reminds me—I really need to get out of here."

"What about you and J.C.?" Hope asked.

Grace grinned at her. "Like I said, I really need to get going. See you around town, Hope."

"Don't think you're off the hook," Hope replied as Grace put her cup in the sink.

"Believe me," Grace replied acerbically. "I'm nowhere near off the hook. Anyway, bring your camera today."

She slipped out of the kitchen, leaving Hope in peaceful silence. With plenty of time to think. Was Grace right? Had she forgotten who the real Hope was? When had she disappeared? And was there a chance she could find her again?

She'd had hopes and dreams once. She'd wanted things—like love and a family. She'd been so sure, knowing that if she had them she'd never let them go like her mother had.

And it hadn't been any one particular thing that had caused her to throw those hopes away. No, it had been a constant chipping away. Every time they moved, every time there was a disappointment or an argument, or every time Hope tried to hold things together and failed. She'd been eighteen and the girls had been teenagers. Of *course* they hadn't wanted to listen to her. But years of insecurity, of little failures, had drained her of energy. Of hope. She gave a bitter laugh. Ironic that that was her name, when she thought of it.

She'd given up hope a long time ago, and her other plans with it. Someone to share her life with. The sound of a child's laughter. Blake had given that back to her, even if it was just for a brief moment. Those kids weren't just his surrogate family, they'd been hers, too, for a very short time.

She went back upstairs and fired up her laptop, sitting at the small desk where she'd once written in her journal and sometimes done her homework. Within seconds she'd brought up the pictures. Looking at Blake's laughing face during the hockey game made her both smile and feel weepy. She clicked through each image. Each one was attached to a memory. The picture wasn't always perfect but the memory was. The boys unlacing their skates. The farmyard during a snow flurry, with flakes softening the edges of the barn and the trees. Anna in her apron, holding a casserole in her hands.

Hope hadn't even looked at the ones from the party— just copied them to the disk for Blake. But she clicked through them now, each one a tug on a tender heartstring. The children in front of the tree, Blake in the middle. The two kids she'd met the first day, sitting together and sharing a plate of cookies. A small boy playing with a new set of toy cars, his grin dominating his whole face.

This *was* Blake's family. She understood it now. This was the reason he got up in the morning. The reason he sacrificed. She blinked. They really were alike, weren't they? They would do anything to make life better for the ones they loved. Except Blake hadn't closed off his heart, had he? She'd accused him of doing that, of not having a family of his own, but he'd opened his heart by choice, to those who needed him.

The final picture popped up on the screen. Blake was holding Cate in his arms with the Christmas tree behind them, its colored lights muted and providing a warm backdrop. Cate's hands rested on each side of his cheeks and above their heads was a sprig of mistletoe. Blake's eyes

were closed and his lips were in an exaggerated pucker as
the little girl kissed the man she clearly idolized.

In all her years of taking pictures Hope had never accomplished it—not until now. But *this* was the perfect
picture. Not because of the lighting or the balance or the
colors or exposure. But because it hit her square in the
heart and squeezed, making it difficult to breathe.

Blake's words—the ones she'd dismissed so easily from
the first—came back clearly, echoing through the empty
chambers of her heart, filling them with bittersweet love.

*"You can't organize perfection. You can't plan it. It just
happens. And when it does, it's magic."*

Magic.

To start with, she'd been in control. At the first sign of
stinging behind her eyes or wetness on her lashes she'd
locked it down—even when Blake had got her talking
about Julie. But it was impossible now, as she stared at
the courageous little poppet and the man who held her
in his arms.

The man Hope had fallen in love with. She was sure
of it now.

Tears rolled down her cheeks as, for the first time since
she was eighteen, she let her heart out of its prison. She
wept for the girl she'd been, and the one she'd become.
She cried for Julie and the loss of someone who'd been
more than a friend. And her heart cracked as she thought
of Blake. He'd seen past it all to the truth of her—something she hadn't even been able to see in herself. And now
he was there and she was here.

She heard again the words she'd said to him that last
night and felt the heavy weight of regret. She hadn't been
fair, and he'd been right all along.

After she'd mopped up her eyes and washed her face,

she picked up the phone in the quiet house and dialed Blake's number.

"Hello?"

It was a woman's voice—probably his mother, already in from Arizona.

"Hello, is Blake there?"

"I'm sorry, he's out. Can I leave a message?"

She paused. What could she say? *Tell him Hope called* was too little. Anything more was too much.

"No—no message, thank you," she said, her voice faltering as she put the receiver down.

She stared at the phone for a few minutes and then took a deep breath. Okay. So it wasn't going to be fixed today. She could accept that. She *had* to accept it. Right now she needed to get ready and head downtown to the festivities, enjoy the time the family had together. Faith would be here later, and after this morning's peacemaking session with Grace it would be good to hang out.

But when she got back she was going to call the airline and switch her ticket. She was going back to Alberta and she was going to face her feelings rather than run away. Everything after that she would take as it came.

The batteries in her camera had run out and a check of the camera bag had come up empty. Rather than stand in line at the drugstore, Hope walked the extra few blocks home to grab a new set.

She'd enjoyed the day. The variety of food had been staggering—including the chowder lunch she'd had at the Steaming Mug. The spiced cider had been piping hot, the decorations had been splendid, and the children's activities had put a smile on her face. And yet it had all left her feeling a little down, too, because each time she saw a couple pass by holding hands she wished Blake were there to share it with her.

He'd love this sort of thing—a real sense of togetherness and holiday spirit. Hope had spoken to the few journalists in town, covering the events, and she was proud of what J.C. and Grace had accomplished. Grace was a writer and Hope took pictures. It was better late than never—maybe they could do something together about Beckett's Run.

She shut the front door behind her and heard the porch board squeak beneath her feet. Smiling, she'd turned to go down the steps when she saw someone standing at the end of the driveway.

She looked up and everything in her body seemed to drop to her feet, then rebound to fill her whole body with joy.

He came.

Blake Nelson was here in Beckett's Run, dressed in boots and jeans and a soft sheepskin jacket and his *hat*. The brown cowboy hat made him seem impossibly tall and, yes, even a touch exotic, and she swallowed, thinking he looked absolutely gorgeous.

Anything she'd thought of saying to him deserted her. All her apologies were jumbled in her head. All her proclamations seemed small and paltry next to the reality that he'd flown all the way to New England on Christmas Eve and shown up on her doorstep.

He took a step through the snow, and another, and when he was close enough for her to hear him clearly he stopped.

"I don't want to fix you," he said.

The air stilled between them, carrying only the faint sound of music coming from downtown and the soft plop of clumps of snow dropping off cedar branches.

"I don't want to fix you, Hope. I love you just the way you are."

It was like she could suddenly hear the "Hallelujah Chorus" in her head. She slowly dropped her camera bag and went down one step, then another. He took one step forward, then a second. A smile blossomed on her face and she was rewarded when he smiled back, slightly sideways as his scar pulled at his lip. It didn't matter. She adored the roguish tilt to it.

When she reached him she stopped and tilted her face up to his. "You came."

"I had to. I shouldn't have let you go in the first place. It was all wrong from the moment you left. I knew I'd made a terrible mistake."

"So you came after me?"

He put his gloved hand on her collar, squeezing the inside of her shoulder. "It was high time someone did."

Oh, he *did* get it! She threw her arms around his neck and pulled him close. It had been so long since she'd felt she was first in someone's life.

"It wasn't trying to be perfect that made me put up walls," she whispered, holding him tight. "It was wanting to feel like I mattered. No matter what I did I never felt like anyone thought I was important enough to waste time on. Never thought anyone would ever think enough of me to stay, you know? Gram was the only anchor I had."

"Now you have me," Blake said softly, wrapping his arms around her. "No matter what happens between us, Hope, you'll have me. Because I know you matter. You matter to me. More than you can imagine." He gazed into her eyes, his wide and earnest. "I didn't say it right that night on the sleigh. I'm not sure I'll say it right now. I know you're scared. I know this is crazy. But I didn't expect to feel this way. You were right. I don't even think I knew I was doing it. I was afraid. I *am* afraid. Of loving someone so much and losing them."

"So what changed?"

"You drove away and I'd lost you anyway. Lost you and missed out on all the wonderful things we might have had. I couldn't let you go—not when I'd found what I'd been looking for all along." His throat bobbed as he swallowed. "I realized that you need to hang on to wonderful things in life with both hands when you have the chance. So they don't get away."

He gripped the sleeves of her coat in his fingers and gazed deeply into her eyes.

"With both hands."

"Oh, Blake."

He wasn't sure of her. She got that now. And why should he be? She hadn't been sure herself until this morning—until she'd been without him and seen the reminder of all she'd left behind. She stood on tiptoe, feeling utterly feminine for once, and not like the awkward beanpole who'd been too shy to take the initiative. She tilted her head and kissed him. Really kissed him—without hesitation, without reserve. He angled his head and her hand bumped his hat, knocking it to the ground, but they didn't stop. Not until the kiss had settled from a question into a certainty. He could be in no doubt of her feelings now.

"We can make it work," he said, holding her close. "I know we can somehow…"

"I was going to change my ticket this afternoon anyway," Hope said, grinning. "I was going to come back after Christmas. I wasn't sure what would come after that, but I knew that yesterday couldn't really be goodbye."

"You were?"

She nodded. "I had a rather interesting conversation with my sister this morning. She told me I was using my job as an excuse to avoid intimacy. She's right. My feelings for you scare me. But I don't like who I've become, Blake. You did fix me—or at least you started to while I was with you. You reminded me of things I once wanted but had given up on. Family. Closeness. A house full of children. And presents and get-togethers."

"You want those things?" He leaned back and looked into her face. "But you always hung back."

"It seemed easier not to hope at all rather than continually be disappointed," she replied. "But I was just pretending to be something I wasn't."

"When you were standing in the kitchen in that apron with flour on your nose I knew," he said. "You belonged there. I didn't know how to make you see it. But you looked happy. It seemed right."

"It was right. You gave me the greatest thing of all, Blake. Acceptance. *You* accept people. Yes, you try to fix them—not to make them someone different from who they are, but to show that they arc already valuable and worth your time. I love you, Blake. I didn't expect to, and I certainly didn't want to, and I wasn't even sure I could. But I do—so much. You're my Christmas miracle and I wasn't even looking for one."

His eyes sparkled at her. "Hope? I want to kiss you again, but we're still in the middle of your grandmother's yard. And if this town is like most small towns then nothing is private. Do you suppose we could go inside, where it's warmer and more…um…?"

She took him by the hand and led him up the porch, over the squeaky board, and inside. He immediately swung her about until she was in his arms and he was kissing her—without the caution of that first time by the tree, and not in the lazy way they'd kissed in the snow, or even the desperate, unsure way they'd kissed only minutes ago in the yard. This one was deliberate, confident. Like coming home and Christmas morning and all the good, fine things she could imagine rolled into one.

When it broke off they were both smiling, and the weight that had been on her shoulders—the one he'd seen right from the beginning—suddenly rolled away. She laughed as she realized she had one final present to give him.

"I finally did it, Blake. I took the perfect picture."

"You did?"

She nodded. "Stay here. I'll show you."

She raced upstairs, boots and all—she'd clean up later—and grabbed her laptop. "I haven't had a chance to print it yet, but look." She brought up the picture and held it out. "It's you and Cate in front of the tree."

"And this is the perfect shot?"

She nodded again, watching his face and not the screen. "It has everything I truly want in it." She took the computer from his hands and put it down. "I saw my mom and dad today. I think they might finally be on the road to happiness. But, Blake, I've realized that I don't want it to take me so long. I want happiness *now*. I want love and a family of my own. Anyone who sees you work with the kids knows you'd be an amazing father. You're kind and loving and you make me laugh."

"Why, Miss McKinnon, it almost sounds like you're proposing."

Was she?

"That might be moving a little too fast," she admitted with a sideways smile, "but Grace was right. I can freelance anywhere. It doesn't make sense to stay in Australia when my heart's in Alberta, does it?"

"Definitely not," he agreed. "So, tell me. What are we doing for New Year's Eve?"

"Still have those sleigh bells?"

He reached out and touched her cheek. "Always," he murmured.

"In the meantime you need to meet my family. Come to the rest of the festival. It's my first freelance gig with Grace. She just doesn't know it yet."

Blake grinned and took her hand.

They stepped outside just as Gram's Christmas lights came on with the timer. In the waning afternoon the yard was transformed into a twilight fairy tale.

She squeezed his fingers. "Merry Christmas, honey."

"I like the sound of that," he replied, tugging on her hand and leading her down the candy cane path.

* * * * *

*Is the Santina-Jackson royal fairy-tale engagement
too good to be true?*

*Read on for a sneak peek of
PLAYING THE ROYAL GAME by USA TODAY
bestselling author Carol Marinelli.*

* * *

I HAVE also spoken to my parents."

"They've heard?"

"They were the ones who alerted me!" Alex said. "We
ave aides who monitor the press and the news constantly."
Did she not understand he had been up all night dealing
vith this? "I am waiting for the palace to ring—to see how
ve will respond."

She couldn't think, her head was spinning in so many
irections and Alex's presence wasn't exactly calming—
ot just his tension, not just the impossible situation, but
ie sight of him in her kitchen, the memory of his kiss. That
lone would have kept her thoughts occupied for days on
nd, but to have to deal with all this, too…. And now the
oorbell was ringing. He followed her as she went to hit the
isplay button.

"It's my dad." She was actually a bit relieved to see him.
He'll know what to do, how to handle—"

"I thought you hated scandal," Alex interrupted.

"We'll just say—"

"I don't think you understand." Again he interrupted
er and there was no trace of the man she had met yes-
rday; instead she faced not the man but the might of

Crown Prince Alessandro Santina. "There is no questio
that you will go through with this."

"You can't force me." She gave a nervous laugh. "W
both know that yesterday was a mistake." She could hea
the doorbell ringing. She went to press the intercom but hi
hand halted her, caught her by the wrist. She shot him th
same look she had yesterday, the one that should warn hir
away, except this morning it did not work.

"You agreed to this, Allegra, the money is sitting in you
account." He looked down at the paper. "Of course, w
could tell the truth…" He gave a dismissive shrug. "I'r
sure they have photos of later."

"It was just a kiss…."

"An expensive kiss," Alex said. "I wonder what th
papers would make of it if they found out I bought you
services yesterday."

"You wouldn't." She could see it now, could see th
horrific headlines—she, Allegra, in the spotlight, but fc
shameful reasons.

"Oh, Allegra," he said softly but without endearmen
"Absolutely I would. It's far too late to change your mind.

* * *

Pick up PLAYING THE ROYAL GAME by Carol Marinel
on November 13, 2012, from Harlequin® Presents®.

HARLEQUIN *Presents*®

When legacy commands, these Greek royals must obey!

Discover a page-turning new Harlequin Presents®
duet from *USA TODAY* bestselling author

Maisey Yates

A ROYAL WORLD APART

Desperate to escape an arranged marriage, Princess
Evangelina has tried every trick in her little black book
to dodge her security guards. But where everyone else
has failed, will her new bodyguard bend her to his
will…and steal her heart?

Available November 13, 2012.

AT HIS MAJESTY'S REQUEST

Prince Stavros Drakos rules his country like his
business—with a will of iron! And when duty demands
an heir, this resolute bachelor will turn his sole
focus to the task….

But will he finally have met his match in a world-
renowned matchmaker?

**Coming December 18, 2012,
wherever books are sold.**

celebrating 15 YEARS

Love Inspired

USA TODAY bestselling author

JILLIAN HART

brings you the final installment of

◄— TEXAS TWINS —►

Twenty-five years ago Dr. Brian Wallace and Belle Colby
were married with two sets of twins—toddler boys and
infant girls. Then the young family was torn apart. Each took
a girl and boy and went their separate ways—never to see
one another again. Brian is stunned to return home from
a mission to find all the siblings reunited at their mother's
Texas ranch. Will unanswered questions stand in the way of
this family finding their long-awaited second chance?

Reunited for the Holidays

Available November 13
from Love Inspired Books!

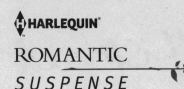

HARLEQUIN®

ROMANTIC
SUSPENSE

Get your heart racing this holiday season with double the pulse-pounding action.

Christmas Confidential

Featuring

Holiday Protector by **Marilyn Pappano**

Miri Duncan doesn't care that it's almost Christmas. She's got bigger worries on her mind. But surviving the trip to Georgia from Texas is going to be her biggest challenge. Days in a car with the man who broke her heart and helped send her to prison—private investigator Dean Montgomery.

A Chance Reunion by **Linda Conrad**

When the husband Elana Novak left behind five years ago shows up in her new California home she knows danger is coming her way. To protect the man she is quickly falling for Elana must convince private investigator Gage Chance that she is a different person. But Gage isn't about to let her walk away…even with the bad guys right on their heels.

Available December 2012 wherever books are sold!

www.Harlequin.com

HRS2780